Lost in the Labyrinth

Other Graphia Titles

A Certain Slant of Light
by Laura Whitcomb

Zen in the Art of the SAT: How to Think, Focus, and Achieve Your Highest Score
by Matt Bardin and Susan Fine

I Just Hope It's Lethal: Poems of Sadness, Madness, and Joy
collected by Liz Rosenberg and Deena November

Open the Unusual Door: True Life Stories of Challenge, Adventure, and Success by Black Americans
edited by Barbara Summers

Owl in Love
by Patrice Kindl

The Road to Damietta
by Scott O'Dell

Zazoo
by Richard Mosher

The Fattening Hut
by Pat Lowery Collins

Lost in the Labyrinth

A NOVEL BY

Patrice Kindl

GRAPHIA

an imprint of Houghton Mifflin Company

 Published in the United States by Graphia, an imprint of Houghton Mifflin Company, Boston, Massachusetts. Originally published in hardcover in the United States by Houghton Mifflin Company, Boston, in 2002.

www.houghtonmifflinbooks.com

The text of this book is set in Gill Facia.

Library of Congress Cataloging-in-Publication Data

Kindl, Patrice.

Lost in the labyrinth : a novel / by Patrice Kindl.

p. cm.

Summary: Fourteen-year-old Princess Xenodice tries to prevent the death of her half-brother, the Minotaur, at the hands of the Athenian prince, Theseus, who is aided by Icarus, Daedalus, and her sister Ariadne.

[1. Mythology, Greek—Fiction. 2. Ariadne (Greek mythology)—Fiction. 3. Theseus (Greek mythology)—Fiction. 4. Daedelus (Greek mythology)—Fiction. 5. Icarus (Greek mythology)—Fiction. 6. Minotaur (Greek mythology)—Fiction. 7. Crete (Greece)—History—To 67 B.C.—Fiction.] I. Title.

PZ7.K5665 Lo 2002

[Fic]—dc21

2002000406.

ISBN-13: 978-0618-16684-8 (hardcover)

ISBN-13: 978-0618-39402-9 (paperback)

Manufactured in the United States of America

POW 10 9 8 7 6 5 4 3 2 1

To my parents, Katy and Fred Kindl,
remembering days in Crete

Contents

Lost in the Labyrinth

Ariadne, Descending

Last night I saw my sister, who is dead. She stood at the end of a long corridor, weeping.

I did not know her until I drew near. There are some here in the Labyrinth who are strangers to me. I thought her a new servant beaten for disobedience, and I looked at her closely only when she did not move as I approached.

Her body was just beginning to be big with child, a child who never saw the light of day. Her neck was encircled by the rope with which she had hanged herself, yet her face was not distorted and discolored, as the faces of the hanged are, and I could see her features clearly.

"Can it really be you, Ariadne, come back after all this time?" I whispered.

She did not answer, but began slowly to sink through the floor.

CHAPTER ONE

Knossos

"XENODICE! COME TO ME THIS INSTANT OR I WILL SLAP YOU! Come this very moment!"

"Yes, Ariadne," I said, dodging from behind a large oil jar. "It is I, Xenodice. I am here. What is your will?" I removed a large cobweb from my elbow.

"Get me some figs. Not last year's figs, but this year's. Nice, plump, fresh figs, newly gathered. You might gather them yourself, Xenodice."

I tried to refuse, knowing full well that it was useless. "Our mother the queen," I pointed out, "has forbidden us to pick the new figs. Indeed, she has threatened us with terrible punishments if we go anywhere near the figs."

"That," said Ariadne, "is why I want *you* to do it."

"Oh, but Ariadne!"

My other sisters and brothers each had a slave girl or boy whom they occasionally treated in this way, but nothing seemed to please my sister Ariadne so well as to torment me, her own flesh and blood. She was nearly two years older than I, sixteen to my fourteen on that spring morning. She never ceased to hold that one year and ten months' seniority over my head like a double-bladed ax poised to strike.

When we were small we had been playmates, and she had often been my defense against the rough play of our older brothers. Now she considered herself a young woman and me a child, and she summoned me only when she wanted something. As always, when Ariadne said "Go," I went, and when Ariadne said "Come," I came.

"I won't do it," I said now, without much conviction. She narrowed her eyes.

"Don't pinch!" I cried. "I'll do it — I will indeed, Ariadne!"

There are a hundred thousand eyes in and about the Labyrinth, and the orchards of the queen do not go unwatched. This was the spring fig crop, the fruits fewer but larger than those of fall. They were doubly precious because we all, palace folk and commoners alike, had been eating old, dried figs for many months. Yet by the goodness of the Lady, to whom I whispered a hurried prayer, I was not caught gathering the fruit, though my heart trembled like a bird in my throat all the while.

Ariadne ate so many figs that I thought she would be sick, but she was not. We had both known that in the end

I would do whatever she commanded. I argued only to prevent her from taking me entirely for granted.

"Let's go and see Asterius," she next proposed. "He would like some figs, I am sure."

"But it's time for our dancing lesson," I said.

"I only suggested it because *you* are so fond of him," said Ariadne. "You always say that I am not good enough to our brother. And now that I wish to do him a kindness you throw up all sorts of objections. You are cruel, Xenodice."

"I am not," I said hotly. "Why do you want to go, anyway?" Ariadne loved dancing lessons, at which she excelled.

She shrugged and walked on. "I told you."

"You merely want to get me into trouble with our mother," I said, trotting along behind her. "She'll not be angry with you; I will be the one to suffer. We could go to our dancing lesson now and see Asterius when it is over. It isn't necessary to go —" I realized with resignation that we were already late for our lesson. The scent of hay and the sound of buzzing flies informed me that we were nearing that portion of the Labyrinth that housed my brother Asterius.

My brother, Asterius.

It is difficult to know what to say about him to you

who do not know him. He is very strange. We are used to him and he does not surprise us. When envoys come to our mother's court from Byblos and Lukka and the faraway land of Egypt, they always ask to see her peculiar son. And when they do see him, they are horrified. I do not like to be present when they first catch sight of him.

He is not clever — how could he be? — but I think that he grasps some idea of the way they feel from their expressions. He lifts his massive head, scenting them. And he groans. His groans frighten the envoys, but they break my heart. I think that he suffers when our mother allows strangers to look at him. Once a year she causes him to be displayed before the whole court during the bull dancing ceremonies, and afterward he seems to go almost mad for several days. I wish she would not do it.

Ariadne says that I am a fool. She says that of course our mother wants him to be seen; it helps to prove that the Queen of Kefti is more than mortal. What mortal woman, after all, could have given birth to such a son? Nothing like our brother Asterius has ever been seen before.

All of this is true, of course, but still I think it unkind.

I have heard that the Athenians, those who come here to be his servants, call him the Minotaur. I do not know why. It means "bull of Minos." King Minos is my father, but he is not the father of my half-brother, Asterius. How, then, is my brother the bull of Minos? It makes no sense.

I think it is because those Athenians believe that men are everything and women are nothing. When they first come here they think that it is my father who rules this land and not my mother, which is remarkably stupid of them. Why would the Lady Who Created All Things allow a man to rule our land? Men have not the gift of creation; they have many talents, but that is not one of them. No wonder the Athenians are poor and ignorant savages who know no better path to glory than to pillage and destroy the civilizations of others.

My brother Asterius stood alone inside a light well, staring up through the five stories of the Labyrinth to the sky. His attendants, those selfsame Athenians of which I spoke, sat a little way off on sacks of grain and bales of straw, playing games of chance and arguing among themselves until they perceived us, whereupon they stood and saluted us. The girls, I noticed, had made chains of flowers and draped them about my brother's head and neck. A flower chain had caught on his left horn and hung crookedly, making him look ridiculous.

I stepped forward, clapping my hands angrily. I pointed to the ring of flowers, which dipped down over his eye. "Take it off," I ordered.

To my fury, they did not immediately obey but looked to Ariadne for instructions.

"Yes," she agreed. "Take it off. He looks as though he has drunk too much wine."

In any event, they did not have to bestir themselves. Hearing our voices, Asterius wheeled about and trotted toward us. Or toward me, rather. He frisked about me for a moment, making those soft grunting sounds of his that expressed pleasure and contentment. Then he held out his cupped hands, begging for the treat he knew I had for him. I dropped one of the fruits into his palm and simultaneously snatched the silly floral decoration off his horn.

Ariadne ignored him, as he ignored her. She was staring at the Athenians, I realized.

There were thirteen of them, too many to serve my brother's simple needs, so they were often idle, as now. There had been fourteen, seven boys and seven girls, when they sailed into Knossos Harbor a year ago, but one of the girls died of an inflamed stomach during the last rainy season. Their time of service in the Labyrinth was nearly over. They had learned a few words of our language and something of our ways. Soon, perhaps even today or tomorrow, another shipload of Athenians would arrive and our mother would give these as servants to various noble houses that had deserved her thanks over the year. Possessing an Athenian servant from the Queen's Labyrinth was a matter of considerable prestige, I believe; people fought to deserve the distinction.

Ariadne looked her full on our brother's servants and then abruptly demanded to know if I would ever be done playing with Asterius. "We are very late for our lessons," she said severely, as though our tardiness was my fault rather than hers. "Leave off fondling that creature and come along."

Annoyed, I turned my back on her and gave my brother a leisurely scratch behind the ears. At last I stopped and indicated that I was ready to leave. But I thought about the Athenians and wondered why Ariadne seemed so curious about them.

Our mother received more youths in tribute each year from Athens than I would have thought necessary, although it was true that as Asterius matured he was becoming harder to manage. Ariadne, who knew everything, had explained.

"She demanded one Athenian child for every year of our brother Androgeus's life at the time he died," Ariadne said. "She was mad with grief when he was killed. She declared that even if the Athenians had offered each year a mound as high as a man of silver and gold, ebony and ivory, bolts of finest linens and silk, she would not have taken it in payment for his death. She might have been satisfied with the death of the firstborn child of the King of Athens, but Aegeus had no child, either first or last. And so she has received each year seven maidens and seven youths, and those the most beloved of their families."

"I know that. I was there when it happened," I protested.

"You were a baby," said Ariadne. "You don't remember anything. You don't even remember Androgeus."

"I do! I remember him perfectly well. And if I was a baby, then you were a baby too."

"Oh, no. I am two years older, and I remember."

"A year and ten months older!"

"A year and ten months makes all the difference in the world," she said pityingly.

To speak the truth, Androgeus is only a faint memory to me. He lives in my mind as a bright and shining image, a memory of warmth and laughter, and that is all. He died when I was two years old. But Ariadne was less than four, so I do not see how she could remember so very much more.

Perhaps you are becoming confused about my family. I must confess that there are many of us, and we all seem born to lead remarkable lives. My mother raised ten children. Androgeus was first born and best loved. They say that he could charm the birds from the sky and the sun from a cloud. He was a golden child, merry and clever, strong and brave of heart. My parents both doted upon him, my father as much as my mother.

He died by the treachery of the Athenians while a guest in their country, and when my father heard of it he laid waste all of Athens. My mother, Queen Pasiphae, then required that seven sons and seven daughters of Athens be sent as tribute each year. I also know that she blamed my father for taking her beloved son away from her and then leaving him to meet his death at the Athenian court. She never afterward forgave him, although she at length accepted him again as her husband and consort.

I have heard it said that Androgeus died on the horns of a terrible wild bull. The Keftiu are a people much preoccupied with bulls, and to me it seems a fitting death for a son of our royal house.

Ariadne no doubt knows the whole story, but I will not ask her. Once upon a time she would have told me had I wished to know. But now she would only tease me with her knowledge and my lack of it. Someday I will hear the servants speak of it, and then I will know without troubling Ariadne.

After Androgeus, Acalle was the second born. She is twenty-two years old if she still lives. She disappeared half a year ago — some say she ran away with the King of

Libya, some say with a god — and we have not seen her since. Everyone was furious, as Acalle was to be queen when our mother died. Now Ariadne will be queen. Still, Acalle may come back someday. I tremble to think how angry Ariadne will be if Acalle returns to claim the crown.

Next in age are my brothers Deucalion and Catreus, who are twins, seventeen years old. Ariadne is sixteen, I am fourteen, my brother Glaucus is seven, little Phaedra is three, and Molus, the baby, is one.

If you have been keeping count you know that is only nine children, not ten. I have not forgotten my brother Asterius — I could not do that. He has just turned twelve years of age. He was born, Ariadne says, nine months to the day after our mother heard about the death of Androgeus. Our father, Minos, was far away, sacking Athens, on the day that Asterius was conceived. He could not be Asterius's father. Indeed, no one who looks at my brother Asterius could ever believe that his sire was human. Our mother, says Ariadne, was so angry at our father for the death of Androgeus that she swore to make another son who would bring shame and sorrow down upon Minos's head so long as our father lived.

I do not like to think about it too much, myself.

But I love my brother Asterius. I always have, ever since I first saw him. I was only three and did not understand how odd he was. He was a young thing who needed nurturing, like a puppy or a kitten. Our mother could not feed him; she almost died at his birth. Once they had taught him to suck cow's milk from a little pottery jar fitted with a sponge, the servants sometimes allowed me to nurse him. He would butt up against me, knocking me down in his eagerness.

"Bad, bad!" I would cry, and the servants would roar with laughter as I pulled myself upright by his tail, holding the jar imperiously out of his reach.

No one laughs anymore; they fear him.

It worries me to see how strong he grows. He is terribly powerful now, and as he grows toward adulthood he is subject to fits of moodiness and intermittent rages. It never happens when I am near, but I cannot always be near. And someday even I might not be able to control him in one of his passions.

I am the only one who loves him. He needs me, you see.

I do not fear him; I fear *for* him.

"If you do not come away this very moment, Xenodice, our mother will have us *both* whipped, and I have no intention of letting that fat Graia lay one finger on me," said Ariadne.

"Oh, very well," I said, and, bidding our brother goodbye, I followed in Ariadne's train.

CHAPTER TWO

Icarus

WHEN I WAS A SMALL CHILD I DETERMINED THAT I WOULD never marry if I could not have Icarus, son of Daedalus and Naucrate, as my husband, and so I think to this day.

I have not yet had the courage to inform my mother, or Icarus himself, of this decision. I did tell Ariadne, who laughed.

"You, a royal princess of Knossos, marry the son of a palace workman and an Athenian slave? Our mother will give you in marriage to a wild goat before she lets you marry Icarus."

I was a fool to speak of my love to Ariadne. I spoke as a child does, a child who still believes that what she wants she must have.

"Daedalus is no common palace workman!" I protested. "He is a distinguished inventor and artist. And Naucrate was a wise woman whose counsel our mother valued."

"Oh, and what marriage settlements could we expect your husband to make? Of what political use would such a marriage be? Don't be such a baby, Xenodice. Leave Icarus to the goldsmith's daughter. She has had her eye upon him for some time."

Not the goldsmith's daughter alone, as Ariadne knew quite well. Nearly every woman in all of Knossos had at one time or another found her eyes turning toward Icarus, as flowers will turn toward the sun.

He was so beautiful! I am not myself beautiful, but it is a trait I admire in others, particularly in men.

Ariadne's gaze had strayed in his direction not a year ago, though she might not be pleased to know that I was aware of it. Everything that concerned Icarus concerned me; I had therefore seen and noted every step of her infatuation with him. I watched her as she came upon him sleeping on a wall one day, his black curls spilling down the stones, his body washed with sunshine. She stood silent for a long moment, contemplating perfection.

Thereafter she was attentive to him, trying to engage him in conversation. He had responded as he always did: he was gentle and courteous, but his eyes were remote. I knew the very moment when she began to doubt her power to ensnare him, the moment when she decided that he was beneath her notice because he did not notice her.

Now Ariadne's unusual interest in my brother's servants gave me an excuse to seek Icarus out and talk to him.

He was himself more than half Athenian, though one of us, a Keftiu, by birth and training. His mother, Naucrate, had been an Athenian woman, a slave. Minos, our father, had given her to Daedalus the inventor in recognition of his skill, and Daedalus, half Athenian himself, had loved her and married her. It was therefore natural that Icarus would understand the language and customs of my brother's servants.

I lay in wait for him by the paint-grinding shed, where he often did work for his father.

His face lightened when he saw me. If he did not love me as a man loves a woman, he did at least like me.

"Hello, little mouse," he said, smiling.

"I am the Princess Xenodice," I said, "You should not address me so."

"No?"

"No. And you should stand up and salute me properly. Icarus, why do you suppose that Ariadne is so interested in the Athenians? Not the ones that are coming, but the ones from last year." I told him of Ariadne making us late for dancing class in order to inspect them. "What is she up to, do you think?"

"Perhaps it is because your mother has promised that Ariadne may choose one as her personal servant when the new lot comes in," Icarus said. He shook several small charred animal bones out of a leather sack onto his work-table.

"Oh! Has she?"

"I am not certain, but that is what they believe," he said. "They have been arguing amongst themselves about which one she will pick."

It was reasonable. Any of them would be pleased to be the trusted servant of the next Queen of the Keftiu. The work of such a one would be light, his bed soft. For the ambitious, there was also the possibility of great political power in the palace.

"And when do the new ones come? Do you know?"

"If you run down to the harbor right now you may see their sail approaching," he said, beginning to grind the blackened bones with a stone pestle.

"Is that true, or are you saying it to be rid of me?"

"I am grieved that you think I would be so discourteous, Princess."

"Icarus!"

He smiled. "To tell true, my lady, I don't know. They will be here soon: today, tomorrow, perhaps in three days' time. I cannot say what day they left, or what winds they've had. There will be plenty of excitement making ready for them down on the wharf. I thought it would amuse you to see it."

As if I were a spoilt child whining for entertainment!

Standing here so close to him as he worked, observing him, and listening to his voice was the only entertainment I could ever want or need. His beautiful, strong fingers were growing smudged with black, I noticed. Making paints for his father meant that yellow, blue, or brown pigment often discolored his nails and stained his hands. I watched for a few moments longer the flexing of the muscles in his arms and back as he worked and then tore my eyes away.

"Yes, well, if you think that the ship will be here soon, perhaps I shall go and look for it," I said reluctantly. I always left Icarus long before I had drunk my fill of his company. I could not bear for him to wish me gone.

But he had forgotten me during that brief silence; his mind was far away and only recalled to me by an effort of will.

"Do, little one," he said absently.

Then he spoke again: "I dreamt of the Athenians who are coming. I dreamt that they rode toward us on the gales of a great storm. And one in the ship commanded the storm and bade it bear them along."

"Oh," I said. For want of anything else to say, I asked, "What . . . what did she look like, the one who ruled the winds?"

"It was a man, a young man barely older than myself" (Icarus was sixteen, Ariadne's age). "He seemed — very sure of himself."

"A man!" I said, surprised. "How should a man use weather magic? Your dream makes no sense, Icarus."

Icarus smiled at me again, coming out of his abstraction. The sweetness of that smile completely unnerved me; I had to cling to the paint-grinding table for support.

"You're right, little mouse, little bird. Not all dreams tell true. When I was done dreaming about unnatural male magicians from Athens, I commenced to dream another dream, one even less likely."

"What dream was that?" I asked uneasily.

"I dreamt —" he paused a moment, then shook his head. "It doesn't matter, Princess. Dreams are nothing but colored shadows in the mind. I cannot believe they tell the future, whatever the priestesses may say."

I frowned and bit my lip. I wanted to know his dream.

"When the ship does arrive," said Icarus, "you shall question the captain yourself and prove to me that no man has learnt the mastery of the winds."

"I will," I promised him. I could see that he was humoring me, and also that his dreams weighed more with him than he would admit. I longed to be able to tell him that these were false images. I did not like the look of secret happiness on Icarus's face when he spoke of the second dream. Jealousy bit deep into my heart; I did not think he dreamt of me.

"Perhaps the captain awaits my interrogation even now," I said, and with a familiar twist of grief in my chest I walked out of the paint-grinding shed. I didn't look back.

As I walked down toward the harbor I passed the cages of the menagerie, which was almost a second home for me. I spent as much time as I could spare helping Lycia, the chief keeper. I fed the animals, talked to them — I even occasionally did servants' work by mucking out kennels and cages. I was happy there; it was my refuge in good times and bad.

Now my favorite monkey, Queta, spotted me and indicated with an imperious cry that she wished to accompany me. As I opened the door of her cage she shrieked with delight and leapt to my shoulder.

"Bring her back soon, Princess," said Lycia. "She'll be hungry and thirsty before long." Queta was still a young monkey and needed frequent nourishment, like a human child.

Icarus was right about the preparations for the ceremonial reception of the new Athenian servants. Carts of potted plants were being wheeled into place and the pier posts decked with wreaths of greenery. Every idler in Knossos Town milled about, pretending to have work to do on the wharves so that they might be present when some sharp-eyed person first spotted the black sail.

Queta was excited, her hair standing up in a fluff all over her body and her tail stretched out rigid as a poker behind her. I held tight to her leash; monkeys do not like large, noisy crowds. Queta might decide she would prefer to observe the scene from atop a fifty-foot carob tree rather than from my shoulder, and then Lycia would be angry with me.

We found a spot on top of a wall where we might watch the jostling crowds without being jostled ourselves, and there we perched while the sun slid slowly down her track in the sky. Queta grew bored with the spectacle before us and occupied herself with picking through my hair, pretending to find and eat nonexistent lice. At length, grunting softly to herself, she curled up and went to sleep on my shoulder. I sat unmoving, lulled by sunshine, thinking of Icarus.

I saw my brothers Deucalion and Catreus being carried by on a litter above the crowd. They were twins, born out of my mother within a few moments of eath other. Like many of that kind, they seemed born with but one soul between them; they had little use for anyone outside their charmed circle of two. They had chosen two pairs of twins to bear their litter so that the onlooker was given the uneasy sense of looking at both reality and its reflection. My brothers were as usual talking to each other and did not notice me.

"Princess Xenodice!"

Someone else had spotted me, however. It was Graia, the bossy old woman who had tended me from my cradle, with little Phaedra trailing behind her and the baby Molus in her arms. "Get down from that wall and go at once back to your quarters. Dress yourself properly. You look like a bag of old rags."

"I do n —" I began protesting, when I looked down and caught sight of my dress. Straw clung to the hem from my visit to Asterius, and a great streak of yellow ocher recalled my visit to the paint-grinding shed. Furthermore, a combined aroma of monkey urine and perspiration from my efforts in dancing class wafted up to my nostrils.

"And bathe," Graia said. "Come. I will see to it myself."

She would have taken me by the ankle and dragged me off of the wall by main force had she not a healthy respect for Queta's teeth. Queta did not care for people laying hold of me and forcing me to do things. As my sister Phaedra now began to object to being removed from the scene of so much excitement, Graia resigned herself to not overseeing my ablutions.

"Very well. I see I must stay here. Tell that worthless girl of yours to stir herself up and do something for a change." She wrinkled her nose. "And make sure she uses some perfumed oils in that bath."

"But I want to be here when the Athenians arrive," I protested.

"No doubt," she said. "That event may happen anytime from now until midsummer. There will be plenty of time to make yourself presentable. And, Xenodice, when you return, have yourself carried on a litter. You are growing too old to run wild like this."

Queta, roused from her nap, was scandalized that Graia should speak to me so. She stood up on my shoulders, gripped my hair by the roots, and began a long, vigorous scold.

"*Aii!* Queta, don't *pull* so!" I clapped a hand to my damaged scalp as I slipped down from the wall and began to trudge up the road to the palace again.

Having returned Queta to her keeper, I obediently searched out my slave girl, Maira, and directed her to prepare my bath. I had argued with my nurse, fearing to miss the arrival of the Athenians, but in my heart I knew she was right and that they might not come for days. And besides, like all my race, I dearly love a good bath.

When I encounter people from other nations, either down at the harbor or formally at court, it is difficult to avoid coming to the conclusion that foreigners, whatever their station in life, invariably stink. They don't seem to realize it, either. Elegantly dressed ambassadors will smile and bow and lean over me, patting my hand in a kindly way, all the while blasting out such a stench of rotted teeth and unwashed bodies that I must fight the urge to flee.

Ours is a society much addicted to washing. Our bathing facilities are renowned all over the civilized world. No one has devised a more elegant and ingenious method of cleaning the body and carrying away its wastes, and I do not believe that anyone ever will. The Queen of Egypt has not a bathroom so fine, even though it is said that she bathes in asses' milk and honey for the sake of her complexion.

I am especially fond of my own bathtub. Well, to be truthful, it is not mine alone but belongs to my sisters as well as myself. Icarus's father, Daedalus, made and decorated it for us, and Icarus helped him, though he was but a child at the time. For this latter reason it is doubly dear to me, but I love it mostly because it is beautiful and clever, like everything that Daedalus makes.

Since it is the bathing place for a princess who will someday rule an empire, the bathtub is designed to give information to the mind while the body sheds the dirt and odors of the day. It is a perfect model of our world, or as perfect as it can be and yet retain the shape of a bathtub.

We are the Sea People, or so we are often called. We live at the very center of the world, at the very center of the sea. Painted on the floor and sides of the tub is a map of the sea, with the Island of Kefti in the middle of it and along the rim the lands that border upon the sea. So, after Maira has released rainwater from the catchment reservoir on the roof into the tub, added a basinful of boiling water to make it hot, and poured in the fragrant oils, I climb inside and find myself sitting squarely on my own homeland, on top of a tiny representation of the Palace of Knossos.

As is fitting, my back is to the ignorant Ligurii in the west. (I have heard that still farther west lies an even greater sea than our own, with lands unimaginable lining its shores, but I care nothing for them; that which is not represented in my bathtub does not interest me.) My left arm lies on the northern shores of the sea, from whence come the Athenians and other Hellenes. My left knee presses upon the land of Anatolia, where the Hittites live. My right arm curls about the southern coast: arid Libya, where my sister Acalle is said to have gone.

Far, far to the east, above the drain hole and almost entirely out of the tub, lies Babylon, where they understand the secret pathways of the stars. Nearer, underneath my right foot where it rests on the rim, is the ancient land of Egypt. And scattered across the face of the sea, underneath my body where I cannot see them, are the many colonies of the Keftiu: Kamikos, Thera, Naxos, and others.

Painted dolphins and squid swim in the sea, camels lope across Libya, the inscrutable Sphinx guards the mouth of the ancient Nile — oh, it is a beautiful bathtub!

I have sat upon my mother's throne often, and once or twice worn my mother's crown. Never have I wished to be queen except, occasionally, in my bath.

And yet to be Queen of Kefti is to be queen of the world, or nearly so. We the Keftiu have no rival in the world, save Egypt. Alone among the nations of the eastern seas, we pay no tribute to Pharaoh; we are equals. The Keftiu do not begrudge Egypt her wealth. Why should we, when so much of it finds its way into our storehouses by means of trade?

Our people are makers and merchants. We have small heart for conquest, though we will do what we must to protect ourselves. It is in our best interests that the sea shall be peaceable and free from piracy; therefore, our ships patrol the waters far and wide, punishing those (Athenians, as often as not) who would attack and plunder honest merchants.

But our greatest joy is the making of things: things of beauty and usefulness, things to amuse and entertain, things of power and wonder. We make so many things that in the end we have not room in our houses and temples and palaces for them all, so we ship some of them to neighboring countries. In return, our neighbors send us lumber and metals and precious stones from which we make yet more things: vases and urns and libation cups, medicines, charms and magic rings, ornaments of gold and silver, finely wrought swords and jeweled ostrich eggs.

We the Keftiu are very clever and very, very rich.

CHAPTER THREE

Lost

SOMETHING DREADFUL HAS HAPPENED. MY BROTHER GLAUCUS is missing. No one can tell where he has gone.

Soaking in the bathtub, I heard the beginning of the uproar. I sent Maira to see what was going on while I dried myself off. She returned, wailing and keening as though already mourning his death.

"The poor little boy! He's wandered off by himself. He's surely been eaten by lions!"

"Don't be stupid, Maira," I snapped. "There are no lions on Kefti." Maira came from Anatolia, where these ferocious beasts are often heard roaring in the waste places.

"There is the lion in the Queen's Menagerie," she pointed out.

A chill washed over me in spite of the lingering heat of the day. Glaucus was just such a plump, round little boy who might be expected to appeal to a hungry beast of prey.

"Go and look, then," I commanded.

"Oh, but — what if the lion is still loose, prowling around? I must stay and help you dress, Princess."

"I am perfectly capable of dressing myself. And if," I added meanly, for I was angry with her for giving me a fright, "if you are right and the lion has eaten my brother, he *may* be too full to think of eating you as well."

"Oh, my lady!"

"Go!"

She went.

If truth be told, I was not accustomed to dressing myself and it took me some time, fumbling with the fastenings of my clothes. My very haste seemed to render them stiff and uncooperative. Still, after what seemed an eternity, I was attired and ready to help in the search.

Glaucus had been missing for much of the day. He had not been seen since just after the morning meal, and it was now late afternoon. His personal servant admitted that he had given the boy leave to go down to the wharves at the harbor to watch the stir and excitement of the preparations there but had not accompanied him. Instead, Bas, the servant, had curled up in a corner and taken a long nap. He awoke just before the midday meal and, when Glaucus did not appear (a most unusual circumstance, for Glaucus was fond of food), began cautiously to inquire about him around the harbor. No one could be found who had seen him, and the servant's fears grew, until at length he was forced to admit that the child was lost and to ask for help in finding him.

The Labyrinth is not a good place in which to lose something. It was built with the intention to confuse and confound. It is as much a temple as it is a palace, for it is the dwelling of the Goddess, the Lady of the Double Ax. A hundred winding passageways leading to a thousand and half a thousand rooms ensure that no one who has entered may leave without assistance.

Only a few months before, the feebleminded son of a merchant in Knossos Town had crept into the palace. I do not myself believe that he meant any harm, but who can say? He eluded the vigilance of the guards and penetrated the private portion of the palace for some reason best known to himself. Being lost in the Labyrinth is bewildering for those of normal intelligence — what must it have been like for such a one as he?

I pity him, thinking of his fear mounting as he trod endless featureless corridors that turned and turned upon themselves and finally led to a dead end. I imagine him running down a flight of stairs, believing that at last he was about to break free of the maze, only to be faced with a blank wall and no way out save by the route he had come.

Eventually he happened upon the Bull Pen, where my brother lives. In the extremity of his terror, the madman attacked my brother with a knife. The Athenians did nothing, of course, except to run like so many squawking chickens. When the soldiers came, Asterius was snorting with rage, trampling about the enclosure with blood and foam speckling his arms and chest. The poor fool lay dead, his neck broken.

I could not prevent myself from thinking of this now. What if — what if Glaucus had gone to see our brother Asterius? What if Glaucus had teased Asterius, pulled on his tail, tormented him in some way? Surely Asterius would not —

My heart beating uncomfortably in my chest, I nearly ran to the Bull Pen. It could not have happened, it *ought* not to have happened, with those servants present. Yet no one knew better than I that servants are not always to be relied upon. I could not believe that all thirteen of the Athenians would stand by while their charge tore a seven-year-old child of royal blood to pieces, but still my feet paced faster and faster as I ran deeper and deeper into the maze.

In the Bull Pen, all seemed much the same as on my earlier visit, except that Asterius was asleep amid piles of hay. The servants arose and saluted me.

"He is not here, my lady," said one immediately. "The little prince is not here. The king, he came and asked and we said, 'No, no little boy came here.'" If my father himself had come looking for Glaucus, then the situation was indeed grave.

I looked about for signs that they were lying, but saw none. There was no indication of a struggle, no terrible patch of blood, nothing to suggest that anything but eating and drinking and gambling had gone on here. If Asterius had been involved in anything like what I dreaded, I knew that he would not now be sleeping but still rampaging about, bellowing and pawing at the dirt floor.

Asterius awoke and came to me. Disappointed that I had brought him no gifts of food, he felt inside my pockets and shook his heavy head mournfully. It occurred to me that I had not taken him outside lately — he must be bored.

It was growing ever more difficult to allow my brother the freedom of being outside, away from the Labyrinth. My father claimed, especially after the incident with the fool, that he was likely to kill someone. I had no such fears, but I was not sure I still had the ability to restrain him if he took it into his head to bolt.

Never mind. Once this fuss over Glaucus was over, I'd take Asterius out and see to it that he exerted his limbs to some purpose. I would bring his attendants and — here was an idea — I would ask Icarus to accompany us. I stroked my brother briefly and kissed his broad forehead in farewell.

I debated with myself what I should do next. Many of

those now searching would themselves be lost in the Labyrinth by nightfall. I could see no purpose in adding a missing princess to the miseries of the day. I had grown up within these walls, yes; I had played here all my life, but even I might lose myself in the maze. Every day, it seemed, new rooms were erected. No one could possibly keep track, except perhaps Daedalus, Icarus's father.

I have heard Icarus say that in Athens they believe that Daedalus built the Labyrinth, as though one man could ever have conceived of it, let alone laid stone on stone to erect such an edifice. They wish to believe it, of course, because Daedalus is partly of their blood and they may thus lay a sort of claim to the most remarkable building on earth.

It's laughable, really. Ariadne says that Aegeus, King of Athens, lives in a crude hall of no more than three or four large rooms, a humbler dwelling than we would think proper for one of our impoverished upcountry farmers.

The Labyrinth has been slowly building, rising tier upon tier, colonnade upon colonnade, corridor upon corridor, room upon room, for more than a thousand years. However clever Daedalus may be (and he is very clever indeed), he is only a man, with a man's normal span of years. He is, however, the overseer of new construction and in charge of redecorating some of the suites of rooms, which may be how the story came to be told in Athens. Icarus claims that his father carries the plan of the whole Labyrinth in his head, which is certainly more than I could do.

I therefore determined to seek further news before extending my search. Perhaps Glaucus had already been found and a feast in celebration was even now being prepared. I hurried away to the public rooms, where I might hope to hear tidings of him.

As I descended the grand staircase in the eastern wing I heard voices on the landing below. They were the voices of the two people most likely to be able to give me the information I craved — my mother and father. The news did not appear to be good.

"Well, Pasiphae, are you satisfied?" said my father. I had been about to call out to them, demanding news, but the tone of my father's words checked my steps as well as my voice. I dropped to my knees and so caught a glimpse of them through the turn of the stairs.

"How can you torment me so?" said my mother, her voice cracked and broken. "Can you not see that I am desperate?"

The grand staircase lies open to the sky, in one of the light wells that bring daylight into the deepest places in the Labyrinth. It was therefore easy to see that my mother was indeed desperate. Her usually perfectly arranged hair hung in black snakes down her back, and the kohl lining her eyes was smeared. Her dress was dirty and torn at the hem — she had been down on her hands and knees on the stone floor looking for her child under beds, in trunks, and behind wall hangings. To my dismay, she looked old. She was forty years old, I knew, and had borne fifteen children and raised ten. She had ruled a mighty empire for twenty years. At this moment she looked to be an old, old woman.

My father was, to the uninformed eye, more composed. His plumed headdress and painted robes were in no disarray; the thick black lines painted around his eyes were sharp and unstreaked. But yet there was a whiteness around his mouth and nose that frightened me, his daughter.

"Your grief is your own doing," he said.

"How dare you speak to me so?" My mother drew in a long, shuddering breath. "You who abandoned my Androgeus among the savages, to be butchered by a wild bull! You! You might as well have murdered him yourself."

I longed to hear what had happened to Glaucus, but my father seemed willing to be distracted by this long-ago grief rather than grappling with the fears of today.

"What should I have done, woman?" he demanded. "Would you have had me take Androgeus to war with me? I am the Lawagetas. Where the navy goes, I must go. You know that I was obliged to go and settle the dispute on Pylos. How should I have known Aegeus would prove the traitor?"

"You ought never to have taken Androgeus with you in the first place." My mother's voice had dropped; passion seemed to have drained out of her.

"The boy was of an age to go," my father said, obviously repeating what had been said before, often and often, over the years since Androgeus's death. "He wanted to go. He said he would leap into the sea and follow the ship until he drowned if I did not take him."

"You *men*," whispered my mother, venom returning to her voice. "You are all alike, all of you, from the day you first grow hair between your legs. Androgeus must prove himself a man by going into danger and *you* must take him there. Then he must prove he is a man by fighting a wild bull because that double-crossing Aegeus dared him to and because you left him behind while you sailed off to war. Oh!" she groaned aloud. "Why should a mother love her sons when they are so anxious to seek their own deaths? I cannot bear it."

There was a silence, save for my mother's weeping. I prayed to the Lady that my parents would be kind to each other rather than inflict more pain. But no, my mother went on.

"And now my Glaucus! It was the fault of that Bas, whom *you* chose to care for the child."

"No, Pasiphae." My father's voice was cold. "This time it is you who bears the responsibility. The servant Bas shall be put to death, and the Athenian servants as well. But it was *your* monster who killed *my* son, and you cannot tell me otherwise."

I drew a sharp breath.

"Asterius is not a monster," said my mother. "He is my son just as Glaucus is my son. And he did *not* kill Glaucus."

"Then where is Glaucus?"

"In any of a hundred thousand places. Have you forgotten, Minos, the nature of the palace in which you live? He may yet be alive. Why do you not do something besides making up lies about Asterius? I know how you hate him, but you shall not deprive me of yet another son through your spite and jealousy. What have the seers to say? What has Polyidus said? He is a great diviner. He found my dragonfly necklace when no one else could. What has he said?"

I gathered up my courage to descend the stairs and speak. However angry it made my father, I must speak up for Asterius. I knew he had not harmed Glaucus.

Before I could move, however, there came an interruption.

"My lady! My queen! I came as quickly as I could!"

There came a sound of labored breathing and the jingling and clanking of many gold ornaments. It sounded as though Polyidus had indeed run all the way.

"My friend, Polyidus!" cried my mother. "You have

come to tell me where to find my boy. You have come to return my son to me, safe and sound!"

"I am sure I shall, my lady," said Polyidus, preening himself.

My father's mouth twisted with distaste. He disliked Polyidus, I knew. I did not blame him. Polyidus *was* a great diviner, but I thought him a creeping, crawling slug of a man. So, I believe, did my mother in her heart, but at the moment she would have been gracious to anyone who could give her hope.

"I must go and get my accouterments, my dear queen," Polyidus said. "The tools of my trade, you know. And then I assure you it will be but a few moments until we find the child, quite unharmed. Will you not repair to the throne room and wait for me there?"

"No. Can't you — can't you just make do with what is here?" my mother said, abruptly moving out of the range of my sight. I descended a few steps to see that she had gone out into the courtyard. "Here is sand that you could use, or pebbles, or water," she said, gesturing about her. "I beg of you, hurry."

"Well." This set Polyidus back on his heels. He liked to have a great deal of ritual and formality while he was working. "I don't know —"

"The Goddess abides in me, as her priestess," my

mother reminded him. "You may draw on her strength through me."

As there was no help for it, Polyidus gave in. "As my queen commands," he said plaintively, following her outside into the open air.

I crept down the stairs and joined a group of courtiers and servants who had gathered around to witness the divination. My mother and Polyidus stood by a pool of water with scarlet fish swimming in it. Polyidus was looking about himself, at a loss. "Now, I suppose I could —" he began doubtfully.

My mother cried out.

A large, golden honeybee had lighted on the first finger of her right hand.

"It is a sign," Polyidus said quickly, before anyone else could give voice to the obvious. "They are holy creatures."

At this, the bee flew away into the palace.

"Follow her!" commanded Polyidus, as though we needed to be told.

Down many halls we walked. As our queer procession moved forward, we gradually picked up more and more people in our train. Hushed, tense, we followed the honeybee, which paused here and there upon a wall, allowing us to catch up, then flew onward in what appeared to be a purposeful manner.

We were nearing some of the humbler portions of the

palace. We walked into a kitchen, shocking the cook nearly senseless. She dropped to her knees, her wooden spoon clattering to the floor beside her, as the queen, leading a parade of great ladies and lords, passed through her lowly domain. "Your Majesty! My lord!" the cook moaned, prostrating herself before us. My mother stepped briskly over her, her eyes fixed on the bee. The rest of the party followed suit. In the hall outside the kitchen, the bee stopped in its flight and landed on the floor. We halted and stared at the tiny animal.

"What does it mean?" my mother whispered.

Then we saw. The bee was crawling on an iron ring. It had landed on a trapdoor leading to one of the storage rooms.

"Oh, quickly, quickly," moaned my mother.

The trapdoor was flung open, and several servants jumped down inside. The bee flew straight to one of the great pithoi, storage jars higher than a tall man's head and broader than his out-flung arms. On the pithos the bee rested.

"In there," said Polyidus triumphantly.

When at length the massive jar was tipped on its side and the contents poured out on the floor, they proved to be three in number: an enormous quantity of honey, a dead mouse, and my brother Glaucus, likewise dead, drowned in a vat of golden sweetness.

CHAPTER FOUR

And Returned

I TURNED MY HEAD AWAY, HALF FAINTING WITH HORROR.

The crush of people pushing forward to see nearly knocked me off my feet — I would surely have fallen if not for a hand that reached out from the crowd and steadied me with a firm grip.

I looked up to see Icarus's anxious eyes on mine.

"Come away, my lady," he said. "You ought not to be here."

I looked back and saw my wild-eyed mother and my stone-faced father standing motionless, staring down at the body of my little brother as it lay in a pool of honey at the bottom of the storage room.

"My parents," I said. "I must —"

"You are better elsewhere, Princess."

I shook my head. "My mother may want me," I said, resisting as he tugged on my hand. "I will not fall," I assured him, and, indeed, I did not believe that I would. There was a sickness at the pit of my stomach, but that was nothing.

He nodded and turned his attention back to my parents, who were now descending the ladder into the lower room. In the lamplight poor Glaucus glistened all over, like a statue washed with liquid gold.

The bee, which had been forgotten, now flew out of a dark corner and settled on the little boy's cheek. Startled, my parents drew back, loath to disturb the servant of the Goddess.

Then my mother cried out. "It — it is *feeding* on the honey."

My father roared, like an animal, like a wounded bull. He snatched at the bee to crush it between his fingers, but it flew away, up and out of the storage room, down the crowded hallway (all there flinched and muttered charms of protection when its flight swooped near), and into the outer air at last.

When the bee had gone my mother fell to her knees in the little storeroom by my brother's body. She raised up her voice unto the Goddess, demanding to know why the Great Mother should see fit to take this child.

"Have I not been a fitting representative for you here on earth? Am I not a dutiful daughter?" We of the royal house of Kefti were direct descendants of the Goddess — my mother therefore addressed her remote ancestor. "If I have displeased you in any way," she said, her voice choked with rage and grief. "I had rather you took my life than those of my innocent children."

The crowd shifted uneasily as their queen railed at the Goddess.

Finally my mother ceased her reproaches. Her head drooped and she began to weep. She wailed aloud in her pain: "Oh, my boy! My little boy!" She bent to embrace Glaucus. She took him up in her arms, but he slipped from her grasp because of the honey. She wailed again, and my father could not look at her but buried his face in his hands.

"My lady! My queen! This must not be!"

It was old Graia, my nurse, pushing through the crowd. Graia was so very old that she had been my mother's nurse as well, back when Graia was little more than a child herself.

"Move, can't you?" she demanded, prodding several people in the back with a rather sharp-looking pair of scissors, which she must have carried away with her in this emergency. "Someone help me down this ladder to my lady."

Graia's face was very red, I noticed, and she looked angry and loving all at the same time.

"Oh, Graia," my mother said, "Glaucus is dead."

"I know, my darling," said Graia. "And it's a shame and a

pity. But you must come back with me to your apartments to wash away the honey. It isn't right that you should be here like this. Come with your old nurse and I'll take care of you, my dear."

"But Graia, how shall I leave him here alone? I must stay," said my mother.

"Come, child," said Graia. "Others will care for the little prince. Come with me now."

"Graia —"

"Come!"

And my mother came. Never before had I seen anyone make my mother do something she did not wish to do. With only a few backward looks, my mother climbed the ladder and meekly followed her old nurse through the crowd and off to her chambers.

I felt suddenly desolate, watching her walk away. I turned to look at Icarus, longing for reassurance of his concern. But I could see that I was no longer present in his thoughts. He stood with his head to one side, gazing curiously down at my brother's face, as if he sought to surprise the secrets of death.

My father, who seemed to have hardened to rock during the late exchanges, erupted into life again. He swung himself up the ladder with such energetic ferocity that it creaked and groaned under his weight.

"Polyidus!" he called out in a voice like a great clanging gong.

There was an uncomfortable silence, then: "Ah, yes, Sire? If there is any way I could assist . . . ?" Nervously wringing his hands, Polyidus made himself evident at the edge of the crowd.

"You said, did you not, that we would find Glaucus alive and well?"

"I said — I said that I thought so, your Majesty. Goddess knows I certainly *hoped* to find him alive and well."

"Your powers are at fault, seer. You led my wife to believe her son would be returned to her."

"Well, and so he has," Polyidus said, gesturing feebly at the dead child. Then, recognizing that this would not be well received, he stammered, "Th-that is, my king —"

"But dead! Drowned!" roared my father with such force that Polyidus staggered backward as though from a physical blow. Terrified, the seer attempted to fall back into the crowd, but my father was upon him in an instant.

Though more than forty years of age, my father was yet a powerful, active man. He seized poor Polyidus as though the man were made of straw and flung him bodily down into the storage room. Before the seer could scramble to his feet again, my father withdrew the ladder.

"As you were so certain of your own ability to produce a living, breathing Glaucus, you shall share the prince's burial chamber until you have managed to do so." He turned away.

"But Sire, I pray you," cried Polyidus. "Give me some water, some light to see by. Of your pity, I beg it!"

"Give him what he asks," said my father shortly. "Then seal the room and let no one give him aid until my son's life has been restored." He strode away, pushing through the crowd, which fell back hastily before his advance.

My father, I thought, was unjust. It was not Polyidus's fault he was a fool. He had only imagined himself the hero, rescuing the prince and being heaped with treasure by my grateful parents. It would not have occurred to him that events might fall out differently.

I murmured as much to Icarus as we filed out of the hallway and made our way back to more stately apartments of the palace.

Icarus shook his head. "If a fool values his life he should stay quietly at home and not go offering advice to the great and mighty."

"If he were wise enough to do that, then he would not be a fool," I pointed out. I sighed. "I suppose Bas, my brother's slave, is dead by now. I am sorry, though he probably did deserve to die. How glad I am that Ariadne is to be queen and not I. I could never order anyone executed." I shuddered.

Icarus smiled. "The Lady Ariadne will have no difficulty there," he said.

"No, she will not, and a good thing too, if she is to be a strong ruler," I said tartly. Ariadne was my sister. Long ago we had played at dolls and dressup, and even though she no longer seemed to value my company, I loved her as best I could. I would not allow anyone to criticize her, not even Icarus.

Besides, I felt a sudden urge to quarrel with him, thinking to blot out my distress with a scalding good fight. But he would not help me. He merely said, "Yes, your sister has the stomach to be queen. You do not." Then, pausing at the entrance to the royal chambers, he said, "How do you suppose the prince came to fall into the honey?"

"There was a little mouse in the pithos with Glaucus," I said. "He perhaps was chasing it, to make a pet of it. He was fond of keeping small creatures in cages in his room. No doubt he climbed from a smaller pithos nearby to the large one. Then later, after he had fallen in, someone found the trapdoor open and closed it."

Icarus nodded. He lifted his fist to his forehead in salute and left me there, alone.

* * *

When I awoke the next morning I hurried to the passageway under which Polyidus and my brother were imprisoned. It was in my mind to raise the trapdoor and secretly conduct the diviner out of the Labyrinth even though my father had expressly forbidden it. Perhaps it would be believed that Polyidus possessed magical powers beyond those he had ever demonstrated and had vanished through his own skill.

Mine was a foolish plan. I could no more spirit Polyidus away unseen than I could restore Glaucus to life. Others had gathered at the place where the young prince had met his death. A large and appreciative crowd sat listening to Polyidus bewailing his fate through cracks in the wooden trapdoor. Polyidus had not been popular.

Evidently he realized that we were present and listening, for he addressed us.

"Hear me, all of you! King Minos shall be accursed! When my lady Queen Pasiphae discovers what he has done to me, her favorite, the heavens will fall down about his shoulders. And you, you who listen to my lamentations with such glee, you shall suffer also. I tell you, I am a seer and I foresee it!"

The crowd did not appear to be much alarmed by this. His failure to foresee the prince's death had robbed him of credibility. Seemingly aware of this, he ceased his threats and lamentations. The people gathered around the storage room waited, hopefully.

At length he demanded, "What enters this chamber?"

Those above stirred happily at this new development. What indeed could it be?

"A rat," suggested one onlooker. Those around him nodded in agreement. It must be a rat, for what else could have made its way into a sealed apartment?

"No doubt you are in the right," returned Polyidus. "It creeps among the shadows so that I cannot see it clearly, but it is some manner of vermin come to despoil the body, I fear. Take that, thou low and slinking thing! And that, and that!"

There came several crashing thuds from below the trapdoor, as though he were throwing stones at the wall.

A silence followed. Polyidus could be heard muttering something.

"I have killed it," he said aloud in a tone of despair. "My doom is sealed now. May the Goddess forgive me."

The crowd was perplexed. How should the Goddess be displeased by the death of a rat?

When they could bear it no longer, an old man leaned forward and spoke through a crack.

"What is it? What have you killed?"

"A snake," said Polyidus dully.

"He has killed one of the sacred serpents!" someone whispered. After a shocked silence, a few elderly women dressed in black began to wring their hands and wail with great fervor.

"I thought it was a rat!" Polyidus pleaded. "Why, it was you out there who said so!"

"Sacrilege!" hissed the man who had made the suggestion. The old women began to wail louder but were hushed. Nothing so entertaining had happened for months, and the crowd wanted to hear every word.

"See where another comes," said Polyidus.

"Do not harm it," commanded the old man in a quavering voice, "or your fate does not bear thinking on."

"I do it only honor," said Polyidus. "It leaves unharmed."

"Hello, Xenodice — come to see the fun?" inquired a voice at my ear. It was my brother Catreus, with his twin, Deucalion, beside him. "Or hear it, rather?"

"No," I said shortly.

"Oh, well, he doesn't mean fun, exactly," said Deucalion easily. "Though I do think that Polyidus was a fool to have promised to restore the boy to life when he couldn't do it."

"He *didn't*," I protested. "He only said that he was sure Glaucus would be alive and well when he found him."

"That's not what we heard," said Catreus. "We heard he boasted of his ability to draw dead souls back out of the

Underworld and reunite them with their bodies. If you can't do a thing like that, it's not clever to brag that you can to a pair of bereaved monarchs."

"It was only that our father has never cared for Polyidus, so he put the blame on him," I said.

"Well, *we* won't grieve for him, I can tell you that," said Deucalion. "Last year he predicted we would suffer a toss in the bull games, and so we did. We can't help but feel that if he'd only kept his mouth shut we would have gotten off without a scratch. And now he's gone and killed one of the sacred serpents, I hear."

At that moment Polyidus began shouting again, and the twins shushed each other to listen.

"What happens here — ?"

A long silence followed and we all stood awaiting developments.

"By the Sun, the Moon, and the Stars," came a terrified chant from below the floor. "By the name of She Who Gives All and Takes All! By the —" The string of invocations broke off.

Another silence, shorter this time. Then: "What a crawling worm may do, a man may surely do also," he said. Mystified, those assembled consulted one another in puzzled whispers.

An interval followed, and then Polyidus said loudly,

"Awake, young master, awake!" A murmur of satisfaction at this dramatic touch spread through the crowd.

But then from under the ground came a cry. "Mama! I want my mama!" The voice did not belong to Polyidus.

Those closest to the trapdoor now drew back, crushing their neighbors in their anxiety to put distance between themselves and the voice.

"Glaucus?" I whispered. I shuddered, and kissed the amulet that hung from a cord around my neck, for I feared it was his spirit only that spoke. "Glaucus!" I cried aloud in a voice I could scarce command. "Glaucus, is that you?"

"Yes," said Polyidus. "Speak up, my lord. Let them hear your voice."

"Xenodice? Let me out of here," my little brother cried. "It *smells* in here. And the seer keeps poking at me. Tell him to stop. *Why am I so sticky?*"

I pushed forward through the crowd eagerly. Just as I reached the trapdoor and bent to raise it, however, several in the crowd objected. They dutifully tapped at their foreheads with the backs of their knuckles as I passed, but they were frightened and they did not mean to let me touch the iron ring.

"My lady," said one, whom I recognized as a journeyman potter. "It is for the queen to do this thing, or perhaps for the king, as he is the one who shut them up in there. Do not let the young lord's spirit out upon us or it will do us harm."

"Oh, very well," I snapped. "Run and fetch my mother and father. Quickly!"

Catreus stepped forward also. "The rest of you, back away. We must have room here. The queen comes!"

I knelt down on the floor and spoke through the trapdoor.

"Do not be afraid, Glaucus. Our mother is coming to let you out. You must be patient only a little longer."

"Xenodice, now the seer has pinched me."

I could hear Polyidus muttering, "He's alive! Alive! I never would have believed it if I hadn't seen it with my own eyes."

"Polyidus!" I called.

"Princess Xenodice! Do you know what I have done, my lady? I have brought the young prince back to life! I have raised the dead!"

"Yes, and we are more grateful than we can say. But please do not pinch the Lord Glaucus. He is but a little boy recovering from a very upsetting experience."

"I am the greatest seer in all of Kefti," Polyidus said with conviction. "In the world!"

"I am very sure you are right, Polyidus," I said, my heart

sinking a little as I contemplated the likely effect of this on Polyidus's self-love. Still, he had raised my brother from the dead and I must think only of that.

My mother came striding along the corridor with my father at her heels, the excited potter trotting in their wake, gibbering of spirits and serpents and seers.

"Be silent," my mother commanded. "Show me."

The crowd had withdrawn to a respectful distance, whether in obedience to the command or through their own fear I do not know. They flattened themselves against the walls as my parents passed; the close confines of the little kitchen and hallway did not allow them to do more than briefly sketch a gesture of respect.

The potter pointed mutely at the trapdoor.

I bent down to the wooden door, said, "Here is Mother, Glaucus," and moved away.

My mother fixed her eyes upon mine.

"Is it he?" she asked. She looked, if anything, worse than she had last night. She had allowed her women to change her honey-stained clothes, wash her face, and comb her hair, but her aspect was dreadful.

I had opened my mouth to answer when the cry came: "Mama! Mama! Xenodice won't let me out and I *hate* it down here."

"My son!"

My father stepped forward. "Polyidus," he called out in a threatening voice, "if this be trickery —"

"Oh, but it isn't, I assure you, King. Truly. The little boy's as lively as a cricket. I did it. I brought him back to life."

"Open the door, Minos!" cried my mother. "Open the door!"

My father stooped and hefted the heavy door. In the shifting light of a sputtering oil lamp were revealed the uplifted faces of the seer Polyidus and my little brother Glaucus. Glaucus's expression was utterly unlike the one I had seen on his face last night. Then he had looked serene, even beautiful, in his golden glaze of honey. Now he looked like an appallingly dirty, thoroughly disgruntled small boy. In the few brief moments of his new life he had managed to smear dirt all over his hands and face, which had of course adhered to the honey. His hair stuck up in spikes, his brows were knit, his arms were folded across his chest, and his lower lip stuck out belligerently.

"I itch all over, Mama," he said irritably, and demonstrated by scratching himself vigorously.

He was unquestionably, undeniably alive.

A wooden ladder was lowered and Glaucus swiftly restored to his mother's arms, once more spoiling her dress. The years dropped from her like castoff rags. She laughed tremulously and covered his filthy hair with kisses, clasping him to her bosom so tightly that he cried out in protest.

I could not help but wonder, Would *my* return from death give my mother such joy?

Polyidus emerged from the underground in a stately, deliberate manner. He paused at the edge of the trapdoor, smiling benignly at the rejoicing crowd.

"I am but a humble servant of the Goddess, no more," he said, when a momentary lull in the noise level allowed him to be heard. "Do not praise me more than my merit, I pray you."

Polyidus was going to be insufferable, I could see.

CHAPTER FIVE

Bull Rider

"WHEN YOU COME TO CONSIDER IT," I SAID, THOUGHTFULLY chewing on the stem of a flowering orchid, "Polyidus did little to deserve his present good fortune. It was the bee that found Glaucus and the snake that fetched the herb that brought him back to life. Polyidus lies when he says he brought Glaucus back to life."

"The serpent brought the herb, yes," said Icarus. "But it did so to revive the other snake killed by Polyidus's stone. It was Polyidus who, seeing the effect of the herb, placed it upon your brother's face. Had Polyidus not been present, your brother would now lie dead in his tomb."

"But he killed the sacred snake! For that act he ought to have been struck dead on the spot, but instead he is covered with honors. It makes no sense."

We three, Icarus, Asterius, and I, were seated near the edge of a precipitous cliff, looking out over the sea. Or rather, Icarus and I were sitting. Asterius was behind us, galloping around and around in a circle, mad with delight at the sun and the grass and the sweet scented breeze. Now and then he snorted and kicked his hind hooves up into the air in an ecstasy of enjoyment. At intervals he flung himself down onto a mass of vegetation and rolled in it, rising up perfumed with thyme and sage and rosemary. The sea lay spread out before us, like the Lady Potnia's blue robe sewn with glittering jewels. A kestrel, making use of the current of air rushing up the side of the cliff, soared effortlessly skyward to float high above our heads. Bees buzzed sleepily and goldfinches flashed brilliantly in the brush.

Behind us were Asterius's Athenian servants. The Festival of the Bull being so close at hand, they were playing at being bull riders and bull dancers, using a large boulder to represent the bull. As I watched, one of the girls, portraying the bull leaper, somersaulted over the rock. She was caught quite neatly by the catcher, but I turned away, wincing. I had no desire to see her fail — I wanted nothing to spoil the day.

Simply to have Icarus close at hand pleased me sufficiently, but today I had his attention as well. Today he did not fly off into strange lands in his mind as he so often did but sat and gossiped like an ordinary person. It was a perfect day, a day beyond praise. My brother lived again and Icarus sat beside me, laughing and talking.

Now he said, "The flower deserves better treatment, Lady," and took the orchid away from me and tucked it behind my ear. "Don't forget," he went on, "the snake lived to sleep in the sun for another day. It was the fate of Polyidus to save the prince and so he did, with the aid of the bee and the snake."

"But should not great deeds be performed by the great? Should not one deserve one's fate?" I asked.

"No." Icarus shook his head. "Most do not deserve their destiny. Look at the palace slaves. What crime did they commit that they should live in bondage? Look at the Athenians. How is it their fault that their king broke the sacred rules of hospitality and sent your brother out to fight the wild bull?"

"But . . . but," I said, wrestling with this problem, "the monarch and the nation are one and the same being, so her crimes are the crimes of the people. She is the mind and heart of the nation; her people are the limbs. One may lose a finger or a toe or even an arm or a leg and yet live, Icarus, but no one survives the loss of one's head."

Icarus smiled and said nothing. I felt a prick of annoyance. How dare he? I had studied statecraft and he had not. "Aegeus of Athens has suffered for his crime," I went on. "He has no legitimate heir, I am told, and so the throne will go to another house upon his death. There could be no harsher fate for one of royal blood. You would not understand."

"No, I wouldn't," he agreed. "My pity is reserved for his unfortunate subjects. They are torn from their parents at a tender age and shipped across the sea to a strange country to be fed to an unnatural monster. That's what they believe, you know — that they are to be sacrificed to your brother." He smiled at Asterius, who was at that moment holding a large, angry beetle in his cupped hands and sniffing warily at it.

I smiled also, at the idea of Asterius making a meal of one of his attendants. He ate only fruits and grains; he had never tasted flesh.

Asterius looked very well in this open place with the morning sun on his back; he was still strange, but that strangeness had been transformed into beauty. I wished that others — my father, for instance — could see him as he was at that moment. His interest in the beetle had given his face a nearly human expression, and his carriage was graceful, the sinewy chest and arms carried proudly above his four-legged bull's body.

"You do not approve of slavery, then?" I said, returning to the argument. "But Athenians also own slaves, do they not?"

"As many as they can get," admitted Icarus.

"I am sure that their slaves are not treated half so well as ours. And the Athenians who attend Asterius will likely find themselves in positions of much greater power and comfort than they would ever enjoy at home."

"Perhaps, but it will not *be* their home. Oh, Princess," he said, with unusual seriousness, "I know you are right. It is only that I dislike seeing my own people in bondage."

"But they are not your people, Icarus, not really. Your mother came from Athens and your father's father also, but you were born and raised here on Kefti. You are one of the Keftiu," I said jealously, disliking the idea of Icarus belonging to anyone else.

An outraged snort made us swing our heads around to see what was amiss with Asterius.

"Asterius? What is it?" I demanded of my brother. I stood and hastened toward him, for I could tell that he was angry.

I heard a giggle behind a nearby tree and my heart leapt up into my mouth. Asterius heard it likewise and lowered his head.

"No! Asterius, no!"

He charged the tree as I ran toward him. A gasp of terror, then I saw bright dark eyes and a pair of naked arms and legs shinning up the tree. Asterius's left horn missed the child's right foot by a finger's breadth.

This was not a child of Glaucus's age, who knew no better. This was a boy of ten at least, gangling and skinny as a colt. He had attracted my brother's attention by throwing stones at him and was preparing to do so again.

"*Stop!*" I shouted, as loudly as I could. "Throw no more stones!"

It was too late. My brother had been hit in the eye. He clapped a hand over the injured area and roared. The child quaked in the tree and tossed another pebble in Asterius's direction.

His shape rendering him incapable of climbing the tree, Asterius instead began tearing it to shreds with his bare hands. He reared up on his hind legs and wrenched large limbs off the tree, snapping them off at the base. The boy shrank away and tried to crawl higher.

"Go," I shouted to Icarus. "Go and get his attendants to help me."

"I cannot leave you in such jeopardy, Princess. Let me try to distract him."

"He will pay you no heed. Go!"

Sometimes in play I would ride upon my brother's back, like the athletes in the bull games. He never seemed to mind, though I could tell it seemed a strange sensation to him. Never, however, had I attempted to mount his back when he was in a passion.

I now took a firm grip of his lashing tail and pulled as hard as I could in the direction of a large boulder that could be used as a mounting block. His forefeet dropped to the ground and he turned to see who had him by the tail. I was not fool enough to believe that in this mood Asterius would know me. I scrambled up onto the rock, trying not to think how his horns would feel, cleaving my flesh. Releasing his tail, I jumped.

I landed on his broad back with a painful thump that knocked the breath from my lungs. I gripped my arms around his waist and my legs around the barrel of his bull's body. Asterius forgot the boy in this new, unexpected situation; he bucked and kicked furiously. As the world heaved and lurched beneath me, I caught a glimpse of Icarus, his jaw slack in amazement. Madly, I found myself wanting to laugh.

A sudden plunge caused me to bite my lip, and all urge to hilarity left me.

"Go!" I shouted, but I could see that the Athenians, alerted by our cries, had drawn near of their own accord.

Asterius tore my hands from him and flung them away like the frailest of cobwebs. I slipped perilously to one side, clawing at his flank with my fingers. One shrewd twist and I would go sliding to my death under those plunging hooves. By great good luck he suddenly lurched to a halt, apparently overcome by the need to express his rage. He pounded his chest with his clenched fists and bellowed until the woods echoed.

Grasping handfuls of his hide and squirming, wormlike,

upward, I managed to pull and push myself onto his back once more.

"Asterius, my brother!" I called to him. "Do not murder me, I beg of you. It is I, Xenodice!"

He snorted, as if derisively, and began to gallop at tremendous speed around the clearing. He did not attempt to penetrate the dense brush nearby or descend the mountain — the path was steep and rocky. I believe also that the clearing reminded him of his home in the Bull Pen.

The boy, I saw, was still up in the tree, held captive by fear.

Asterius was beginning to tire. He breathed enormously, his sides heaved, his whole body was slick with sweat. His eye was still wild and there was foam on his lips, yet I thought I might tame him. I spoke to him again, my voice firmer this time.

"All is well, Lord Asterius," I said. "We must be calm so that we may travel down the mountain and seek medical attention for your eye." He slowed his pace a little; he was listening. "All is well," I crooned, "all is well."

Gradually he came to a halt. His head swiveled around and he saw me. He shook himself all over, as if to throw off his angry mood, nearly dislodging me as well. I clung to him, however, and even risked loosening my death clasp around his waist to pat him cautiously.

At this moment, the boy in the tree chose to loose his last stone at my brother.

"I'll kill the little beast myself, if I ever get the opportunity" was my last coherent thought as we reared into the air and I clamped my arms and legs about Asterius again.

Icarus and the attendants now reappeared — I realized I had not seen them for a time. I later learned that they had withdrawn from sight behind trees, disliking to interfere while I had him under some sort of control. Now there was nothing to be lost by their presence and everything to be gained. They closed in and flung a net — brought along for just such an emergency — over us both.

Asterius fought against the confining net for some time, until every tooth in my head felt as though it had been jarred loose and the muscles of my arms and thighs were on fire and my wrist, which had been damaged in the struggle, became a torment to me.

At last, at last, he groaned and sank to his knees. Moving swiftly as thought, Icarus sliced a long slit in the net and tried to pull me through it. I had held my position so long, however, that it was difficult to unclench myself. Icarus had to pry my frozen fingers loose and gently drag me away, ever in mortal dread of Asterius's swinging horns.

Icarus tried to carry me away from Asterius, but I

protested. In a weak voice I directed him, "No, let him see me. It may help. We have yet to get him down the mountainside."

Icarus therefore laid me down near Asterius, where I could reach out a hand, still rigidly curled into a hawk's talons, and rest it on his flank. Asterius was ashamed, I could tell. He would not look at me, but hung his head mournfully and lowed like a cow.

I scolded him in a soft voice while Icarus examined my wrist.

"It is beyond my knowledge, Princess," Icarus said. "I do not believe it is broken, but there are many small bones in the wrist, any one of which may be shattered without the fact being obvious. We will have the doctor Asclepius look at it when we return. He is said to be the best in the world, and I know him to be kind and gentle."

At length I thought to ask about the boy in the tree.

"He is gone, my lady," said one of the Athenians, a woman. The servants were squatting on the ground in a circle about us, still panting a bit with their own late exertions. "I looked to see, but he was off and gone by the time I did."

"That boy should be fed to the lion in the Queen's Menagerie," observed another of the servants.

"I nearly agree with you," I said in a shaky voice.

"Certainly *I* would have left the little whelp to his own fate and then said nothing more about it," said Icarus.

"No, you would not," I said.

"No, perhaps not," he concurred. "But now there can be no attempt at hushing this up. Even if," he glanced at the Athenians, "even if we could all be trusted to hold our tongues, there is your wrist. It must be tended and you will not be able to use it for a time. That will cause comment."

I had not got that far in my thoughts yet. Icarus was right. The tale would undoubtedly spread and gain color and volume as it did so. People — most especially my father — would be convinced that Asterius was a wild and untamable beast.

"Could we not —" My eyes traveled around the ring of Athenians and I knew it would not do. They were sympathetic now, but they would not hold their tongues, all the same.

I stood up straight, cradling my wrist, and addressed the Athenians. "We who were here today know what happened. The boy hid behind a tree and threw stones at the Lord Asterius. Only when the Lord Asterius was injured did he seek to harm the boy. I charge you, tell the tale that way. Do not let people believe that my brother attacked an innocent child. As it is," I turned and looked at my brother,

"I fear I will not be able to take him outside the Labyrinth again for a very long time, if ever."

The Athenians nodded and made obeisance to me. Icarus made sure of their word by discreetly passing a few coins about the circle. Soon I stood and flexed my muscles, preparing for the long journey down the mountain. As I moved cautiously about, I guessed that I would be most dreadfully sore when I woke next morning, but save for my wrist, there did not seem any serious damage.

Icarus, who had been watching me, called out, loud and clear: "Hail, Bull Rider!" It was the salute given to those who have successfully ridden the bull in the bull games without falling off or being gored.

The Athenians saluted me likewise, crying in unison: "Hail, Bull Rider!"

Traitorous tears started without warning from my eyes, and my cheeks burned like fire. I bowed briefly, as the bull dancers do, more to hide my face than for any other reason, and then quickly turned to look out to sea.

There was a black speck among the dancing sea lights. It was still so far away that I could not make it out.

"Icarus," I said, and pointed.

His eyes were sharper than mine. "It is the black sail," he said. "My Lord Asterius's new servants come."

Behind me, I heard the Athenians give a soft, sighing cry.

CHAPTER SIX

The Presentation

"YOU BREAK YOUR WORD OF HONOR TO ME, YOUR DAUGHTER and heir, for that posturing ninny?"

I stared at Ariadne, fascinated. I had never seen her so angry. Every drop of blood seemed to have drained from her face. The very hair on her head was alive and waving with fury. Her fists were balled, as though she would strike our mother as she sat on her throne.

"That 'posturing ninny' restored your brother Glaucus to life," Mother remarked calmly, leaning back and studying her daughter. "He deserves a reward. Several rewards, in fact. I value all my children, not my daughters alone."

"Then give him a reward, by all means. Give him land, a house, a ship, whatever he desires, but don't give him *my* Athenian."

Mother's eyes grew cold. "None of the Athenians are yours, daughter. They are mine, to dispose of as I see fit."

"You promised!" Ariadne was now nearly spitting with rage.

I wished I were closer to Ariadne so that I might kick her ankle or deliver a warning pinch to her arm. She was going too far. Ours was a loving mother, but she did not allow disobedience or disrespect from any of her children. As things were, I was too far away, sitting on the floor in a corner of the throne room nursing my damaged arm and playing quietly with Phaedra and baby Molus. The servants who normally cared for them were busy, preparing a feast to mark yesterday's arrival of the new Athenians. Ariadne paid my worried glances no heed.

"I said that you might be allowed to keep one of the Athenians if nothing further came up. Something further has come up. The last Athenian will go to Polyidus." Mother made an abrupt gesture of dismissal. "You may go now, daughter."

Stony-faced, Ariadne executed a sketchy salute that barely escaped insolence in its brevity. She turned and moved stiffly toward the door.

"By the bye, Ariadne," my mother said softly, "you are *not* my heir. Acalle is my oldest daughter."

Ariadne halted, as though a rock had struck her squarely between the shoulder blades.

I closed my eyes and prayed that my sister would keep silent and go.

Praise the Lady, my prayer was heard. Ariadne stood

still for a long moment. Then she walked away without a word.

I regarded my mother with some surprise. She had not the look of a woman who believed her oldest daughter dead or beyond recall; she was smiling a little, unmindful of my eyes upon her.

But where could Acalle be? Had my mother recent tidings of her, that she smiled so? Why not then announce them? Perhaps she had known all along where Acalle was. What if Acalle were absent at her request and conniving? My mother had not wept a tear when this oldest, most precious daughter had disappeared.

"Speak no more about it. She is gone."

That is all she ever said on the subject, in my hearing at least, from that day to this. When one considered the many years of mourning and the vengeance exacted against the Athenians for the death of Androgeus, who was only a boy and could therefore never sit upon the throne, that fact was remarkable.

There were as many opinions on the subject as there were inhabitants of Knossos. Some said that Acalle, like many a royal heir, had grown querulous and discontented, tired of waiting for the day when she would be given some measure of real power, and had therefore been sent away to learn humility elsewhere. Some said she had died of a dreadful disease and been quietly buried. Others said that Acalle had fled south across the sea without her mother's consent.

For several months before she disappeared, the young king of Libya had been visiting Knossos to negotiate a trade agreement. All could see how my proud sister grew red and white by turns whenever he came near. Libya was a poor and desert land. Acalle would never have received permission to marry the ruler of Libya.

But why, if any of these things were true, would we not have heard after all these months?

I myself believed that our mother in her wisdom had discovered a spell aimed at her daughter and heir by some malignant magician and had therefore sent Acalle secretly away to a place of concealment until the spell was counteracted or the magician was discovered and destroyed.

But then, what would happen when Acalle returned? What a whirlwind that would bring!

I found myself hoping that Acalle was happily married, a queen in her husband's land, without designs on the throne of Kefti. I wished her well, but far away. She too was my sister, but, being so much older and the acknowleged heir, we had never been on terms of intimacy. It was Ariadne's happiness that most affected mine.

Ariadne would not be able to bear the loss of the

throne. She had not the temper to accept having high estate snatched away from her. Even this loss of the Athenian slave was a bitter fruit she could not easily swallow.

The keeper of the granaries now entered with a complaint about the way the records were kept, and I decided to remove myself and the children. The need to understand proper accounting practices for all the great store of treasure and goods hidden in the bowels of the Labyrinth was one of the many reasons *I* would not wish to be the next queen. And besides, my wrist had begun to throb, although the doctor Asclepius had given me poppy juice in wine to ease it. Like Icarus, he did not believe that it was broken, only that the small muscles were torn and bruised.

We had been lucky. The arrival of the new Athenians meant that much less attention had been paid to our mishap than might otherwise have been the case. The servants who had been present on the mountaintop would now be dispersed to many households and have other things to think about. And the boy's parents would not speak of it. The child had escaped injury, and Lord Asterius was the queen's son.

So I comforted myself, and so I believed.

"Phaedra, Molus," I said quietly, "let us go to the kitchens and see if they will give us some dates to eat before the Presentation of the Athenians."

"Figs in honey," proposed Phaedra instead.

I shuddered, remembering Glaucus in his thick coating of honey. "No," I said. I picked the baby up with my uninjured arm, and Phaedra and I bowed to our mother and retired. She nodded and went back to listening to the keeper of the granaries speaking in a high, indignant voice about sixteen missing sacks of barley.

We the Keftiu are a people who enjoy celebration. There are many holidays, both major and minor, festive and grave, throughout the year. The Presentation of the Athenians is a modern rite, begun only twelve years ago. Since it is followed so soon after by the Festival of the Bulls, one of the great holidays of the year, it has over the years tended to flow into that celebration. The ritual is a solemn one, being in commemoration of the death of my brother Androgeus.

All of the attending populace wore their best mourning costumes as they gathered in the Bull Court, that central courtyard at the heart of the Labyrinth where most public occasions took place. Years ago, there had perhaps been a little more real grief as well as a good deal less jewelry displayed, but twelve years had come and gone since Androgeus had died in foreign lands, and people could not help but look forward to the festivities of the morrow with a cheerful face.

It might seem odd, this lengthy mourning for the death of a male child, but sons are always useful, and my parents had loved Androgeus dearly. I believe that much of the joy vanished from their lives when he did.

Today, however, both of my parents looked well content. The restoration of Glaucus almost on the anniversary of Androgeus's death seemed to have made gloom impossible. I wondered if this would be the beginning of forgetting for them both.

My mother wore her traditional mourning garments, but like many in the crowd she had decked herself with jewelry, and her eyes shone behind the mask of the Grieving Mother with a brightness not due to tears. My father, I noticed, bent down his head to speak with her, and she lowered her mask and smiled up at him. I could not catch the words, but the tone seemed unguarded and cheerful, as if they were exchanging family pleasantries. My spirits rose and I rocked the whimpering Molus on my knee to quiet him.

The musicians began to play a sorrowful dirge as a sign that the ceremony was about to begin. The crowd, recognizing its cue, groaned and cried and bewailed the death of Androgeus. Those who most hoped for royal favor tore at their elegant costumes. Some fell down on the ground and rubbed dirt into their faces and hair.

The new Athenians entered the Bull Court under guard.

Remembering what Icarus had said, I wondered what this must be like for them. If they believed that they were victims to be sacrificed to some dreadful beast, they would be terrified indeed. All were young, of about my age or a little older. I watched one, a girl with brown hair and small, delicate hands and feet. At first glimpse, I saw no signs of fear, but then as I studied her I realized that she had traveled far beyond fear, into that country where death comes as a welcome friend. I pitied her, and blamed the captain of the ship for not telling these wretched people their true fate. How long and sorrowful the journey must have been!

And now this great, mourning crowd was hardly a cheerful introduction to their new lives. I for one would be glad when the brief ceremony was over and I did not have to think of their dread any longer.

The young woman I had been watching was pushed forward by two guards, each carrying a sacred Labrys, the double-bladed ax consecrated to the Goddess. The Labrys is to be found everywhere in the palace, both in reality and in representation. It is carved, over and over again, into the walls of the Labyrinth. That is what the word *labyrinth* means: "Hall of the Double Ax." The girl stumbled and was steadied by one of the guards. She was made to come and stand before the queen.

Once before my mother, each guard rapped the Athenian girl smartly with the butt end of his Labrys — not the glittering blade end, but the blunt shaft — first on the back of her neck and then on the back of her knees. The rap on the back of her knees caused her to fall prostrate on the floor. It was a symbolic execution, payment for the death of Androgeus. In prior years my mother had received her tribute in silence, motionless behind her mask. Today she nodded her head, as though to hurry the ritual along.

The girl lay motionless for a moment until prodded by the guards. She lifted her head slightly and looked warily about, as though awaiting the final stroke of the Labrys, this time with the blade end. One of the guards prodded her again and motioned her to get up. Slowly she climbed to her feet and lifted her eyes to his. He pointed to a place by the wall away from the other prisoners and she fled, half fainting.

After a few of the Athenians had been thus presented, I thought I could sense a slight lessening of tension among those remaining as they realized that the ones who had gone before had come to no actual harm. They seemed glad enough to cooperate with the guards, to mimic death, since death had passed them by.

The last Athenian, a man a little older than Icarus, was brought before the queen. As the ceremony was so nearly over I turned my attention to Phaedra. After our fright of three days ago, I was determined not to lose her in the crowd as it dispersed. I was preparing to lead her away when a sudden interruption in the ceremony occurred.

The young man refused to fall down. He stood erect before my mother and called out something loudly in his own language. It was not, by the tenor of his voice, either a plea for mercy or a threat of violence. Outraged, the two guards struck at him furiously, over and over again, until he fell.

I took a firm grip of Phaedra's hand and hurried her away, wondering what the man had said. I knew some words of the Hellenic language through listening when Icarus spoke to the Athenians, but these words I did not recognize, and they were pronounced with a mainland accent. He was a great fool if he thought that any words of his would alter his fate, save for the worse. And why, when the others had safely survived the Presentation, did he seek to cause trouble?

That night at the feast, I sought to have myself placed near the captain of the ship that had brought the Athenians. I should have remained at the high table with the royal family, but no one objected. Compared to Ariadne I was unimportant and therefore allowed greater liberty.

I had not forgotten Icarus's dreams, you see, and I wished

to hear them disproved. He had revealed only one to me. That one was ominous enough, and yet I thought that I disliked even more the other dream, the one that made him smile, and the one he kept secret from me. I thought that if one dream were proved false, that would refute them both.

The captain was flattered to be sought out and was soon talking about the voyage.

"No," he said, puzzled. "There was no great storm, Princess Xenodice. The weather is usually untroubled at this time of year. There was a little delay in loading some of the supplies, which made us later than we might have been, but otherwise . . ."

Feeling much happier, I then demanded, "And was there a weather witch on board with you?"

"Well, no. We had the usual charms on bow and stern, of course, as well as several wind catchers on the sail, but no witch. There's not a great deal of space on a ship like mine for passengers. In wintertime, of course, we'd welcome her, but as it was . . ."

"I meant one of the Athenians."

He shrugged. "Frankly, your Highness, I don't know. I don't speak much of that Hellenic tongue. I've got an oarsman who knows it pretty well, and he translates for me when I have need. They're just cargo to me, you understand: I see to it they're fed and watered and none of them escapes or tries to kill himself or anyone else, and that's the end of my interest in them. I have other duties and little leisure to spare."

"Then," I said, struck by another thought, "I suppose you don't know what that young man, the last one to be presented to my mother the queen, said? That was strange."

"Oh, him!" growled the captain in disgust. "I know which one *he* was. Self-important young rooster! If I hadn't known my own life would be forfeit, I'd have tossed that man overboard and slept easier at night. Always talking, lecturing, arguing. My guess is that he's the son of someone important in Athens. Or somebody *they* think is important, anyway. They all look the same to me, even that King Aegeus. They call him 'King,' but he looks more like a dirty, toothless old dog to me."

"Did you see King Aegeus, then?" I asked, feeling some curiosity about the man who had caused my brother's death and so much misery to my parents.

"Not this time, my lady. Other years I've gone to collect tribute he's been there, striding up and down on the shore and cursing and shaking his fists at us, as though the whole thing wasn't his own fault to begin with. He doesn't come too close, I notice — my men are armed. No, as I say, this year I never caught sight of him. They seemed more upset this year. They always are, of course, but this year . . . I suppose that man you asked about was somebody from one of the landed families and that got everybody more riled up than usual."

"But then, why would he be chosen to go? I know my mother demands the best beloved children, but surely that is a mere matter of form by now. Would not the wealthiest houses bribe a poor family into sending one of their children?"

"They choose them by lot, or so I understand. I suppose the rules about cheating are strict. After all, even they must fear the wrath of the Goddess, ignorant savages that they are."

I nodded.

"I tell you what, Princess," said the captain, with the cheerful unconcern of one who has successfully handed over a tedious responsibility. "I don't envy the family that ends up with that Theseus as a servant when his year of palace duty is up. Give me a slave who knows his place and how to keep his mouth shut."

"Theseus?"

"That's right, my lady. If there is one thing I do know about that man, it's his name. He kept saying it over and over all the way here, along with some other gibberish I couldn't understand. 'I am Theseus of Athens!' That's what he kept saying: 'I am Theseus of Athens and Troezen!'"

CHAPTER SEVEN

The Festival of the Bulls

ONCE, WHEN I WAS A LITTLE GIRL, THE GROUND BENEATH THE Labyrinth shifted. Pots and jars fell to the floor and splintered, the roof of a jeweler's studio on the eastern side of the palace collapsed, and several minor fires blazed up where furniture or cloth had fallen into open fire pits.

It frightened me, but my nurse, Graia, assured me that it was nothing. "Only a bit of temper, no more," she said, and she told me this story.

"Deep within the Island of Kefti," she said, "below the deepest caverns, below even that realm where the dead people dwell, down in the darkness and the heat of the earth, there lives a gigantic bull. The Bull in the Earth is the dearly beloved husband of the Lady Potnia, She Who Made All Things.

"The Lady loves her people, the Keftiu, but she also loves the Bull. These two loves do not always harmonize with each other. The Bull is as large as a mountain, and his breath is a roaring flame hot enough to melt stone. If he were allowed his freedom he would surely kill each and every one of the Keftiu. The Lady therefore keeps the Bull pent up within the earth, where he cannot destroy her people.

"Often the Lady goes to visit her lord deep in the bowels of the earth. This is why the people of Kefti seek to honor their Lady by placing offerings inside any of the thousands of sacred caves that thread their blind paths through the roots of our island. We likewise wish to show reverence to the Bull in the Earth. We love him for his beauty and power and we also fear him, even shut away as he is. For when the Lady does not visit her lord for a time, he becomes restive. He turns in the darkness and tosses his horns, and the ground above him quakes and buckles. Buildings crumple and fall, and the fire of the Bull's breath sweeps through the ruins. Many of our people die when the Bull is angry.

"When your grandmother was a girl," said Graia, "the Bull in the Earth grew so furious that much of the Palace of Knossos was leveled. Hundreds died in the wreckage of the Labyrinth, and thousands died in the countryside around, and in the towns and palaces of Malia, Zakros, Festos, and Kydonia. The palaces are rebuilt now, grander and larger than before, but we do not forget."

She explained that since there is little we can do to urge the Lady Potnia to visit her lord if she does not choose it, we perform many ceremonies to appease and entertain the Bull in the Earth, hoping to keep him quiet and amused in the event that his lady should be absent longer than his liking. He is a fierce creature, and his pleasures are likewise fierce. So, several times a year, bulls are sacrificed in his honor amid much ceremony. And once a year, in the early summer, there is the Festival of the Bulls.

My brother Asterius is the son of the Bull in the Earth. They say that my mother, in her grief over the death of Androgeus, begged the Goddess to help her get revenge against Minos for leaving her son to die in a strange land.

She Who Made All Things would not lightly refuse such a request from her high priestess. The Lady therefore entered into my mother's body and took possession of it. As one they descended into the Underworld, where the Bull dwells. And in due course my brother was born, half man and half bull.

That is why my brother appears before the people once a year at the Festival of the Bulls.

The Bull Festival would be very different from yesterday's brief, sad rite of the Presentation. It was a happy occasion and one of my favorite festivals; I looked forward to it the whole year. Nor was I alone in this: all over Kefti young women and men had been preparing their entire lives for the festival, when they would face the bull before the entire court of Knossos.

The bull dance is glorious. However often I see it, it makes me want to weep for sheer pleasure. It is everything in life that is beautiful and brave.

When Icarus and the Athenians hailed me the day before as "Bull Rider," they were being kind. I had performed only the simplest of the feats to be displayed here — that of riding the bull without injury — and I had done so without grace or style. The great bull dancers and those who admire them would have thought little of such an exhibition.

What a crush of people filled the Bull Court! I sat with my family — except Ariadne, who was preparing to perform the Dance of the Serpents for the opening ceremonies — on a balcony off our living quarters. Servants moved silently about, offering barley water and wine, grape leaves stuffed with spiced meats, delicate pastries, and platters of fruit.

The array of balconies around the court were crammed to overflowing. Here and there I could see a familiar face — those places were reserved for people of wealth and influence. Up on the roofs and lining the walls of the actual Bull Court were the common people. They would stand in the grilling sun without food or water for hours today.

Some would faint from heat and thirst and be carried away, allowing others to push forward and take their places. Those in the Bull Court itself were in some danger; the bull occasionally charged the audience. Yet in spite of all this there were always more than could be accommodated. Tomorrow those lucky enough to be present would go home to their villages basking in reflected glory.

In contrast to yesterday, the throng was a blaze of color and fanciful design. Some of the costumes worn were like old friends — I had seen them year after year — but others were new to me, made especially for this occasion. I scanned the crowd, seeking out past favorites and new creations. I laughed to see a man dressed in gray with the mask of a hippopotamus, and then admired a woman with a headdress fashioned like a grove of trees with little silver birds swinging from the limbs. The men wore their most richly embroidered kilts and robes of many hues today, and any woman who could afford a ceremonial dress had it on.

I was dressed in ceremonial attire myself, for almost the first time. These dresses were different from ordinary clothing in that the bodice was cut down low to the waist to expose the breasts. I had only just made blood sacrifice to celebrate the commencement of my monthly bleeding during the last rainy season, so I was still uncomfortable in women's dress before this great crowd. My breasts were small and pointed, like the teats of a nanny goat. Graia said that they would grow, but that was meager comfort today, feeling that everyone's eyes were upon me.

The seer Polyidus had been given a seat with my family, I noticed. Neither he nor Glaucus had been improved by their brush with the mysteries of death. Polyidus sat there grinning and bowing and nodding his head at everything that was said, while my little brother capered about, boasting wildly before the servants.

"Stop, Glaucus," I said, annoyed, as he lurched against me in one of his rough games and nearly tore my dress. "Sit down and be quiet." The monkey Queta — who sat on my lap, securely diapered to prevent her from soiling my clothes — fluffed up her fur and screamed at him.

Mother drew Glaucus to her. "Darling," she said, stroking his hair.

The musicians began to play, and slowly the buzzing, rumbling crowd quieted, waiting.

Ariadne entered first. This was the first Festival of the Bulls without Acalle, and therefore Ariadne's first appearance in her place. She and I had rehearsed and rehearsed her entrance, yet even knowing what to expect I gave a cry of pleasure at the picture she made. From all around me came a roar of delight.

She was masked and gowned to represent the Goddess and mounted on a chariot drawn by a pair of cheetahs. The chariot was so fashioned that golden wings appeared to be sprouting from the back of each of the big cats. The effect was to make them look like the griffins that attend the Goddess and draw her conveyances.

The cheetahs were uneasy. I watched anxiously, fearing that they would bolt. Cheetahs can run fast, faster than any horse. They did not flee but sat down and clawed at the straps binding them to the chariot. I bit my lip and longed to take charge of the chariot myself.

Ariadne, however, had everything under control. She bowed to her mother and to the giant sacral horns at one end of the Bull Court, which represented the Bull in the Earth. Then she turned her attention to the cheetahs. She was firm, wielding her little gilded whip to good effect on their backsides. The procession advanced.

Behind Ariadne and the cheetahs came Lycia of the Queen's Menagerie, keeping a sharp eye on the cheetahs. Then came my brother Asterius, attended by his servants. The gaily colored ribbons tied round his arms and waist and tail were stained with sweat. The crowd cheered loudly on seeing him, and his eyeballs rolled wildly in their sockets. Nervous, he pranced sideways, butting into his attendants. I looked away, not wishing to witness his suffering.

After him came a group of priestesses wearing over their heads and shoulders masks of many animals: a vulture, a fish, a cow. Behind them were the bull riders and bull dancers, liberally decked with flowers, and finally, the tumblers, jugglers, and clowns who would entertain between events. These last did not walk but rather cartwheeled and somersaulted their way around the bull ring, their trained monkeys, pigs, and dogs cavorting merrily among them.

Queta, who had been clucking with alarm over the cheetahs, now uttered a loud *Hoo! Hoo!* on seeing bosom friends and hated enemies from the menagerie in the throng at the tail of the procession. I slipped a cherry into her mouth and she hushed.

When the parade had completed a full circuit of the arena, Ariadne reined in her cheetahs, who promptly lay down and showed signs of wanting to roll in the dust. Ariadne dismounted, and Lycia came forward and led the cheetahs and chariot away, followed by the rest of the participants. I sighed with relief.

Two of the priestesses entered the ring and approached Ariadne, carrying the sacred serpents.

At that moment my mother stood up.

"My people," she said aloud.

As if she had twitched a magic thread, three thousand heads turned to look at her. The audience hastily surged to its feet.

"My people," she said, "it is many years since I have danced the Dance of the Serpents. I will do so again today."

A startled silence ensued, then whispers washed back and forth across the whole expanse of the courtyard like waves in a pond. There came a cry, "Hail, O Blessed Queen!" The crowd took it up and shouted in unison, smiting their foreheads with the knuckles of their right hands in salute.

The queen bent down and kissed Glaucus before descending to the arena. "My son," she murmured, and caressed his cheek.

I understood. She wished to perform the dance to give thanks to the Goddess and to the serpent who had saved her son. But would Ariadne understand? Or would she take it as an insult?

Glaucus flung himself into a seat behind me and began steadily kicking at the legs of my chair. I closed my eyes and tried to feel gratitude for his preservation. When I opened them again I saw Ariadne standing motionless, her face as wooden as the mask she held in her hands.

The priestesses made humble obeisance to their queen. The two carrying the basket with the snakes began to move away from Ariadne and toward our mother, but Ariadne put out her hand to stay them. The crowd fell silent, sensing drama.

Oh, Ariadne, do not do so, I murmured to myself.

After a long dragging moment, while my mother and sister stared at each other, Ariadne withdrew her hand. We sat motionless, watching. Slowly she bowed to the queen, handed her the mask, and then turned abruptly and walked out of the arena. The priestesses gently twined the snakes about my mother's arms and waist and throat and then, taking up their torches, positioned themselves for the dance.

For me, the Dance of the Serpents passed in a haze; I was waiting for Ariadne. As time went by and she did not appear, I became frightened. She must be seen as a dutiful daughter or our mother would be forced to take action against her.

I had determined to go and look for her when suddenly she appeared. To my surprise, she did not look angry but, rather, bemused, as if something unexpected and pleasing had occurred. Her breasts, so much rounder and more womanly than mine, rose and fell rapidly with the stirring of some emotion. Her eyes glittered and her whole body was tense with excitement.

As my mother and the priestesses prepared to leave the court to the bull dancers, someone darted out from the crowd and intercepted them. He bowed deeply and spoke to her. It was Daedalus, Icarus's father.

My mother stiffened. She stood motionless, listening

to Daedalus. She seemed to protest, then nodded curtly and strode out of the arena. When she sat down again with the family, I saw that she was now furious. Two little spots of color had appeared high on her cheekbones.

I looked at Ariadne and then back again at my mother, but the moment of disobedience seemed forgotten by both mother and daughter. Apparently they both had other matters to busy their minds.

Once again I found it difficult to concentrate on the events enacted before me. The bull riders came and went. I stared at their brilliantly colored costumes and antic clowning without seeing. Dimly I noticed when a young bull crashed through the ring of spectators and tried to leap the barrier into the audience, but my thoughts kept returning to my mother and my sister. The audience gasped and applauded, but we three sat silent, unmoved and untouched by events in the amphitheater.

But soon the bull riders were done and the most beautiful and most dangerous part of the ritual had begun. A team of bull dancers entered the arena and all thought was banished; I watched with my whole heart and my whole mind. The dancers positioned themselves in front of the chute from which the bull would enter the ring: three to the left, three to the right, and one in the center, farthest from the chute.

The great crowd grew silent, and it seemed possible to

hear a muffled heartbeat, as if all of our hearts were beating as one.

The music began. A fresh bull was released into the ring. He lifted his head and sniffed the air. Sensing nothing worse than seven nearly naked women and men arrayed before him, he advanced cautiously.

The bull's little piggy eyes were too shortsighted to see the full extent of the crowd that surrounded him, but he could hear it and smell it. He did not like it. He bellowed deep in his throat, dropped his head, and prepared to impale the dancers on his horns. His tail lashed.

At this signal the dance began. The two dancers closest to the bull ran toward him, towing long red streamers that twirled and fluttered in the breeze. The bull, annoyed, pawed the ground and charged. The paths of the dancers intersected immediately in front of his nose, and the trailing banners lapped his body in scarlet. Bucking and twisting, he pulled free of the linen strips, only to find himself facing the second pair of running dancers, then the third. The bare arms of the last couple nearly brushed his horns, but their streamers wrapped around him and he was too confused to lunge.

Behind the third couple, the last dancer, a girl even younger than myself, ran lightly up to the charging bull's head and grasped him firmly by the horns. In one liquid movement she tucked her head down, curled her body upward, and, thrown into the air by the strength of her arms and a furious toss of the bull's head, somersaulted right through his horns. For a brief instant, both bull and bull leaper were suspended in space, he in full stretch leaping forward, she a spinning ball above him.

It was flawlessly executed. One great sigh forced its way from the lungs of three thousand people, like the breath of the Bull in the Earth himself.

Two things then happened at once. Behind the bull, a male dancer caught the bull leaper in his arms, and in front of the bull the remaining dancers ran, madly waving their streamers. Utterly enraged, the bull plunged forward, his hind hooves narrowly missing the leaper and her catcher. He slashed to the right and the left with his horns, and the dancers scattered in all directions. The bull was left alone in the ring, bellowing with fury and deeply confused about what had happened to him.

The crowd went mad with joy.

Each performing team had a different routine, a different method for distracting the bull from the dancers. Most were beautiful, some were comic. When the last group of bull dancers had at last left the arena, my mother stood again and addressed the people.

"I am told that there is one here who wants the opportunity to join in our sport. Although he is a stranger to our land, he has an especial right to do so if he wishes."

The crowd was startled. Foreigners were never allowed to participate in the Festival of the Bulls. And how could an untried and untested stranger hope to survive such an experience?

Daedalus walked out into the amphitheater again, this time accompanied by another man. The man inclined his head slightly and spoke, haltingly, in our language.

"I am Theseus, son of Aegeus, King of Athens. I give you greeting. I claim the right to compete in your games."

I recognized him now. It was the man who had spoken out at the end of the Presentation yesterday. But — how could he be the son of Aegeus? Everyone knew that Aegeus of Athens had no son. I stared at this upstart who claimed to be someone who did not exist, looking at him carefully for the first time.

He was not beautiful, and that was against him, for we Keftiu love beauty. He had none of the lithe grace of a bull dancer but was short and stocky, with thick, knotted muscles. He wore no jewelry or fine attire.

Daedalus bowed deeply before my mother. Theseus did not.

"Hear, O Queen!" said Daedalus. "Before you stands Prince Theseus, son of Aethra of Troezen and Aegeus of Athens. He greets you and asks leave to wipe out his father's blood debt by facing a bull as fierce and wild as the Marathonian Bull that killed your son Androgeus twelve years ago."

"His father seems not to have known of his existence until recently," Mother observed. "Certainly I did not."

"He was reared by his mother in Troezen, without his father's knowledge, my queen," said Daedalus.

Ah! An illegitimate child, then. No doubt his father, lacking any other issue, was now willing to acknowledge him.

The queen considered, and then spoke.

"Your request is reasonable."

The crowd murmured, pleased with her generosity.

"It is fitting that Aegeus's son should pay for his crime. However, the bulls we have here today for our festival are exhausted from their efforts. You will no doubt be willing to remain as a guest in my court until a bull worthy of your strength and courage is located."

As Daedalus translated my mother's words, Theseus's face darkened. He sputtered a bit in his own language and then, stabbing himself in the chest with his forefinger, shouted, "I! I! I do not fight —" He struggled for a moment and then twisted around and demanded the proper words from Daedalus.

"No, do not speak!" said Daedalus. "I will answer for you!"

"I speak!" roared Theseus. "I speak!"

Daedalus shrugged, and after a few moments' consultation Theseus turned back to the queen.

"I do not fight old, tired, tame bulls! I am Theseus of Athens and Troezen, a prince and a hero! The greatest hero of our time!"

The audience looked at him skeptically.

Theseus rumbled, "These animals I see here today are — they have no — they are not manly. They are like cows. I do not fight with cows. I come here to kill the monster and no other do I fight."

The queen lifted her eyebrows.

"The monster?" she inquired.

Daedalus shook his head mournfully. "*Ohi,* Theseus, *ohi.* Do not say it."

"The monster! He who has devoured so many of my people! I kill him. I kill the Minotaur!"

CHAPTER EIGHT

My Father's Son

"THAT WAS THE MOST CONTRARY, HEADSTRONG, *IDIOTIC* YOUNG man it has ever been my fortune to meet," said Daedalus.

When the Festival of the Bulls was over, Ariadne had, without a word to anyone, run down into the arena. Unhappily, I followed her, Queta riding on my head and complaining shrilly in my ear. Ariadne seemed different. I didn't like it, and I meant to see what she did next.

We wended our way through the hordes of departing worshipers and at length caught up with Daedalus, who was striding along on his way to the artisans' studios. It appeared that Ariadne wished to question Daedalus about the man Theseus.

"Surely not idiotic," objected Ariadne.

"Yes, idiotic, Princess. I explained three times that the Minotaur, as they call Lord Asterius, does not eat flesh at all, let alone human flesh. And even in Athens they must have heard rumors that the 'Minotaur' is the son of the queen, *not* of Minos. The fool would barely suffer me to address the queen rather than Minos. And why should he think that either ruler would allow him to butcher their son? He has lost not only his liberty but, very shortly, his life. And all because he would not listen!"

"Oh, but have I not heard you say how different it is over there on the mainland?" said Ariadne eagerly. "How could he know? How could he credit a world in which everything is so altered from all that is familiar to him?"

"Because I told him so," snapped Daedalus. Icarus's father was old — nearly fifty — and the combination of his age and his great value to our queen made him less respectful toward persons of consequence than he should have been.

"Look here, Princess," he said, in a more civil tone. "Let us say that you are a young person but lately departed from your mother's hearth, and that you find yourself at the mercy of one of the most powerful rulers in the world.

"Now, let us suppose that you are the legal and rightful possession of this mighty queen, to be disposed of as she sees fit," Daedalus went on. "And let us also suppose that this queen has every cause to hate you and wish you dead. Why then, Princess Ariadne, if you should ever find yourself in this position, I would advise you to listen very carefully and very gratefully to the counsel of a man older and wiser than you, who is also a distinguished member of your own race and nation." He looked at her under fierce brows.

"That is all I have to say. Good day to you." He caught sight of me behind Ariadne and his manner softened. "Princess Xenodice, you have not been to see us of late. You must not abandon your old friends."

I blushed. It was true enough. I had not stopped by the workshop recently, as I had been able to see Icarus several times in other ways.

"I will come soon," I promised. He bowed and walked rapidly away, obviously impatient to get back to work after a day's holiday. Daedalus could never bear to be idle for long.

Ariadne was silent for a moment when Daedalus had left us. Then she said, "Daedalus's self-love is hurt, that is all."

"Well, yes," I said slowly, "I suppose it is, but that does not mean he was wrong in what he said. If Theseus had followed Daedalus's advice, he would have had a chance to wipe out his father's blood debt and return victorious to his own country. Now he has lost everything, for he might have lived long and well as a slave at Knossos."

"He would rather die than live as a slave, especially here at Knossos."

I looked at her curiously. "How do you know that?" I asked, although I suspected that she was right. Along with the ship's captain. I did not envy anyone who received such an argumentative and quarrelsome servant.

"He told me so," she said, and then tried to change the subject. "And what are you doing following me about, Xenodice?"

"Theseus told you?" I demanded. "How could he have told you anything? He arrived only the day before yesterday and he has been under guard the whole time! When did he tell you?"

Ariadne hesitated. She looked at me sideways from under her lashes. I could see that she was longing to tell me but unable to guess at my reaction.

"When I came up from the processional he was waiting to address our mother," she said. A smile flickered across her lips. "He is very muscular. And *very* hairy."

"Oh, Ariadne, how awful!"

"Not at all. You're a baby. You know nothing about it."

"But how did he come to speak to you?"

"Oh, I spoke to him — I noticed him yesterday. I thought that I would ask Mother to give him to me. She owes me restitution for giving my slave to that imbecile Polyidus."

She fell silent for a moment, her face sullen, clearly meditating the ways in which our mother owed her. Then she said, "I do not believe that I will *ever* forgive our mother for taking the Dance of the Serpents away from me in front of everyone that way."

Hastily I explained why I thought that Mother had chosen to dance the Dance of the Serpents in place of her daughter.

"She's too old," Ariadne said spitefully. "Her belly wobbled. Everybody was laughing at her; she looked like a fool. If she had let me do it as she ought, *I* could have given thanks to the Goddess for the preservation of Glaucus. I am the eldest daughter now and it is my right."

"But Ariadne," I said, startled into contradiction, "no one was laughing at her! People were — they were *pleased* to see her dancing after so many years."

"Oh, shut up, Xenodice!" She was suddenly furious. "Just go away and leave me alone!"

The light in her eye was one I knew all too well. Notwithstanding our elegant attire and the sacredness of the occasion, all that preserved me from assault were the sharp teeth of the monkey perched on my shoulder.

"Very well, Ariadne," I said, backing up a few steps. I reached up and stroked Queta, who had gone rigid at Ariadne's tone and was no doubt making threatening faces. But even my valiant friend Queta might quail before Ariadne, I thought. Ariadne had the spirit of a tigress.

As I left, however, I could not resist asking one last question.

"You spoke with that man before he addressed the assembly. Did you mention that the 'monster' was your brother?"

She looked away without replying.

"*Did* you?"

"No."

"He knows now," I said, watching her face.

She reddened, and stamped her foot at me. I retreated, thinking. I had always known that Ariadne disliked Asterius, but it had never occurred to me that it was shame that she felt.

Although I never cared to think overmuch upon my brother's begetting, I had never felt any embarrassment about him. Indeed, as Ariadne herself had pointed out, he was an asset, proving our family's close link with the Goddess. And in any case, I loved him; he was my brother.

"Father! Wait!"

A boy of about ten years suddenly shot out of a doorway across my path so that I nearly stumbled and fell. Annoyed, I turned to look and discovered that it was the child who had thrown stones at Asterius on the mountaintop two days ago.

What evil chance had allowed the boy into the palace on this of all days? For one brief moment I glimpsed the figure of a cloaked and hooded man, who dodged around a corner ahead of the boy.

On impulse, I followed them and found myself hurrying down a small, winding corridor that led toward the offices of the scribes, where much of the day-to-day business of Knossos was done. It was quiet here — few were at work on this great holiday.

It seemed queer. There had been thousands of strangers in the Labyrinth today, true, but why should one be lurking in this out-of-the-way place, and why did he not wait for his son? There was something furtive about his movements.

I ought to have called a guard, but I did not know for certain that the man and his boy meant any harm. In truth, my concern was partly for them — they might so easily become lost in this deserted part of the maze.

"Father!" cried the boy again. "Please wait! I cannot run so fast." He turned a sharp corner and, unseen, spoke again.

"Father! Father, is it true? Will that man really kill the monster?"

Indignant, I was about to plunge in after him to inform him that no, that man would *not* be allowed to kill my brother, when another voice spoke.

"Yes, my son," the man said, and the sound and timbre of his voice halted me like a fist in the chest. "The Athenian will kill the monster for you, though I cannot."

Unbelieving, I stood motionless, listening. My utter stillness warned Queta, who sat mute on my shoulder.

"Why can't you?" the boy demanded petulantly. "Why can't you kill him for me? You are the king!"

The man was my father.

"I am the king, yes," he said, "but the queen is the living flesh of the Goddess here on earth. If I lifted my hand against her son, who is also the son of the Bull in the Earth, not I alone would suffer for it, but you as well, Eumenes."

"It's better to have the Athenian do it then," agreed the brat.

With the blood pulsing in my ears, I turned and walked quickly and silently away. I knew — I had known for years — that my father had had relations with women other than my mother. Ariadne had told me so, though I would have been much happier to remain in ignorance.

This, then, was a child from one of these unions. An image of the boy's face flashed across my mind. I had to admit that his eyes reminded me of the twins, Catreus and Deucalion. The boy who had thrown rocks at Asterius was my half-brother, just as Asterius was my half-brother. How strange!

Father had always hated Asterius, and now he had further reason. The boy had no doubt told his father — *our* father — about the day on the mountainside, making it seem that he had been viciously attacked. But Theseus was a prisoner, and now doomed by order of my mother the queen to die. How could he possibly do any harm to my brother?

I walked faster. If I told my mother what I had just heard . . . No, I could not. It would be dreadful for my family. My brother would be safe, but what would my father's fate be? And after all, perhaps my brother was in no danger.

A persistent odor informed me that Queta badly needed her diaper changed. I returned her to a keeper in the menagerie and then hurried to the royal apartments. I found my mother preparing for her bath, surrounded by her attendants.

"Mother," I said, catching at her elbow as she stepped out of her gown. "Mother, tell me, when does the Athenian prince die?"

Mother looked annoyed. "Do not try to save him, Xenodice; you are too tenderhearted. Theseus is his father's child indeed! He comes to my court and announces that he means to kill yet another of my sons! But do not grieve over him. His death will cancel out Aegeus's debt. It is just — a son for a son."

I raised the knuckles of my fist to my forehead in

salute. "Your benevolence is great, O Queen," I said formally. "But I did not seek to save the man Theseus. I only wished to know when he would die."

She looked up sharply and motioned her women away.

"You wished to know —! Is this my sweet-natured little daughter, she who cannot bear to crush an insect? *Why* do you wish to know when the young man dies?"

My head drooped; I stared at my feet. Never before had I desired another's death. But now I was frightened. I did not know the precise nature of the danger, but my forebodings centered around this young Athenian.

"He threatened to kill Asterius," I said, sounding no older than Father's boy. "I am afraid for my brother."

"Oh, if that is all! Do not fear, he cannot escape. And if he could, how could he find your brother, and, having found him, how could he kill him unarmed?"

"Someone — someone could help him," I suggested.

"No one would dare. Better still, no one would wish to do such a thing. Now, stop worrying this instant. Do you know, I was rather afraid at first that you had fallen in love with the man. You're growing up so." She looked at my small pointed breasts. When I blushed, she laughed. "I'm glad to know that's not so."

"Oh no, Mother. He's such an ugly man."

"Well," she said, musing, "I wouldn't call him so. Some women find men like that quite attractive. But evidently you don't and that's all to the good. Now go and leave me to my bath."

"But Mother," I protested, "you didn't say when —"

"No, I didn't and what's more, I won't," she said good-humoredly. "Don't worry, little one. Asterius is quite safe from the son of Aegeus."

And with that I had to be content.

Theseus was not executed the next day, or the next. The court in those days after the festival seemed stretched tight, waiting. After having eaten and drunk and danced and sung our fill we ought to have returned to our every-day lives. What, then, were we waiting for?

This tension seemed to center around the queen my mother. She laughed often these days, which was uncommon for her. She teased her little slave girl and gave her presents of sweetmeats and a small gold chain for her ankle. And every morning and every evening she climbed up to the lookout tower, the highest place in the Labyrinth, and stared out over the sea.

Two days after the Festival of the Bulls, our mother summoned Ariadne to her presence in closed conference. When Ariadne came out of the throne room, she was seething and smoking like a pot of oil left overlong on the fire. After that I avoided her whenever I could.

The very next day, however, she demanded that I accompany her to Daedalus's studio.

"He likes you," she said in explanation. "He'll tell you things."

"What sort of things?" I asked, suspicious.

"Come *on*, Xenodice," she said, pulling me ruthlessly along.

Icarus was seated on a windowsill of the untidy room, gilding the horns of a rhyton carved in the shape of a bull's head.

"Oh, it's only you," said Ariadne, disgruntled.

"Yes, my lady, it is only I," he agreed, standing to salute us and holding the rhyton away from his body so as not to smudge the paint.

"That's rather nice," she said, looking at the rhyton, which would one day hold the blood of a sacrificial bull.

"It's very beautiful," I amended, because it was.

"Thank you," he said tranquilly and waited to hear what we wanted. I could tell that he was having one of his dreamy, otherworldly days. Ariadne could tell, too. She looked as though she wanted to shake him.

"Where is your father?"

"I cannot say, Lady. Not here. He left some time ago without telling me his errand."

Ariadne looked exasperated. "Still," she muttered to herself, "perhaps *he* knows." She whispered urgently in my ear, "Ask him!"

"Ask him what?" I whispered back, bewildered.

"Where Theseus is imprisoned, of course!"

"But — but why —?"

"Never mind why — just ask him!"

"*Aii!* Ariadne, that hurt! Why don't *you* ask him?"

"Because — just *ask!*"

"I don't want to, Ariadne. I don't want to know, and I don't see why you should, either."

Icarus put the rhyton down on the window ledge and waited.

Ariadne released me. She pulled herself up to her full height and said, "Icarus, I *command* you to tell me where the man Theseus is imprisoned."

"I do not know, my lady."

Ariadne hissed in frustration.

"But," Icarus continued, "my father knows."

"Does he? How do you know?" she asked eagerly.

"Because I heard your royal mother Queen Pasiphae tell him to make sure the prisoner was incarcerated in the deepest, most secure chamber at the very heart of the maze. Which chamber that would be I cannot say, but my father could."

"He could, but *would* he, that's the question," mused Ariadne aloud.

Icarus's attention was drifting back toward the rhyton.

Apparently forgetting our presence, he held it up to the sunlight, admiring the line of fire reflecting down the golden horns.

"You could work it out yourself, I suppose," Icarus said absently, picking up his paintbrush.

"What do you mean? How?" Ariadne demanded, staying his arm before he could dip the brush into the golden medium.

He laid the brush down again.

"The oldest section would be the deepest, wouldn't it, my lady?" he said. "They built the present palace on top of the ruins of the first. And then, our queen said that the chamber should be at the very heart of the maze. The Bull Court is at the very heart of the maze." He turned back to the rhyton.

"Wait! Put that stupid thing down for a moment. So what if the Bull Court is at the heart of the maze? You can't keep a prisoner in the Bull Court!"

"You could keep a prisoner in a room under the Bull Court, though," Icarus said.

"But there are no — Icarus! Are there rooms *under* the Bull Court?"

"I have heard my father say so, Lady."

"Then that is where he is. But how shall I find my way there? And how shall I know which is the proper room?"

"I cannot say. But you might watch the kitchens for the servant who —"

"Icarus," I said uneasily, "do not —"

"— who is bringing him his meals, for he must be eating," Icarus concluded.

"Icarus, you are brilliant! Every bit as clever as your father!" Ariadne's face lit up with joy. There in Daedalus's workshop she began to dance, closing her eyes and moving her body with a fierce concentration.

"Thank you, thank you for this boon, Great Goddess!" she cried. Still gyrating, she left us.

"Icarus, how could you?" I said.

"He is the son of my father's cousin," Icarus said, and he went on painting the bull.

CHAPTER NINE

Theseus

IT WAS NOW THREE WEEKS SINCE THE FESTIVAL, AND THESEUS had not yet been executed. My mother was waiting and watching for something, some signal, before she had him killed.

I had taken to spending a great deal of time with Asterius. In this situation I could not depend upon his servants to defend him; they would naturally be on the side of their prince, Theseus. Indeed, they might themselves be a danger to Asterius.

I did not take him out to the mountains again but brought my distaff and spindle down into the Bull Pen. I sat in the light well, in the shaft of sunshine that penetrated even into the subterranean Bull Pen, and there I spent my days twisting flax into thread. Whenever Graia wished to be free of the care of Phaedra and Molus I brought them there as well and saw to it that my father heard of my new habits.

"How industrious you are, my daughter," he said, staring hard at me. "But you should be dancing as well as spinning. You are the daughter of a queen."

"I do not dance so well as I spin," I said. "And I enjoy spending time with my brother Asterius."

"Take very good care that my little Molus and Phaedra do not annoy their brother Asterius. He is a wild and violent creature, and I would not have my babes harmed. Indeed, perhaps it would be better —"

"I will take care, my father," I said hastily. Luckily a messenger came for him bidding him to the queen's presence before he could prohibit me from bringing his children to the Bull Pen. I knew that their presence there was the best method I could contrive to ensure the safety of Asterius.

And so I sat and so I spun. My clew of thread grew long and longer still. I called for flax and yet more flax. The injury to my wrist was luckily on the side holding the distaff and not on the side that spun the spindle; even as it was, both wrists ached from the task.

All day I spun and into the night, stopping only when the flickering light of the oil lamp made the flax strands seem to twist and wind by themselves without the aid of my spindle.

Ariadne discovered me in the Bull Pen, spinning as usual.

"Xenodice, come away," she said. "I need you to do something for me, and you *must* do it. You must!"

"But I don't want to leave. What is it?" I asked.

"Xenodice, you have grown very stubborn lately," Ariadne said. "You do not show me the respect due to an elder sister and one who will someday be a queen."

"I am sorry, Ariadne."

"What are you going to do with all that thread, anyway?" she demanded, staring at the large and ever-growing ball.

"One can always use more thread," I said. "Perhaps I will have it woven into a new dress."

"Well, put it down now. I do not wish to speak before all these people." She waved her hand at the Athenian servants. "Or before the brats." She scowled ferociously at Molus, who began at once to whimper.

"Very well," I said reluctantly. "But you will have to wait until I find Graia and deliver them into her care."

"Oh, don't fuss so," she said. She swept us all three out of the Bull Pen, giving me no time for more than a backward glance at Asterius, who watched our departure curiously. "Here, you!" She flagged down a passing soldier. "Take the Princess Phaedra and Prince Molus to their nursemaid."

The soldier and the two children regarded each other in dismay.

"Yes, my lady," said the soldier, presenting his weapon and saluting her. Molus burst into tears.

"Ariadne, I really think —"

"Come with me now, Xenodice!" Ariadne said through gritted teeth. "I mean it. You are the only one in the world who can help me."

She dragged me up the staircase to the third floor and into a deserted state bedroom. Drawing me as far from the doorway as possible, she clasped me about the wrists with cold hands. I winced with pain and attempted to withdraw my injured hand.

"My wrist — it pains me," I said.

She shifted her grasp to my elbows and fixed me with a long stare.

"You must help me. I will die if you do not." She shook me in her vehemence.

"Help you to do what?" I asked uneasily.

"Set Theseus free, of course. Don't be an absolute idiot, Xenodice!"

"I'll not do any such thing!" I said.

"What do you mean?" she said, taken aback. "Of course you will. I'm telling you, you must!"

"How could you ask me to do such a thing? And why should you want it?"

"Because I love him," she said.

"Because you —! No, I don't believe it!"

"And why not?" she demanded.

"Oh, Ariadne," I cried before I could stop myself, "he is so ugly!"

"He is not!" She released my arm and snatched up a lock of my hair. "Do not say so! He is not ugly."

"He is!" I shrieked recklessly. "And most likely he smells, too! *Aii! Aii!* Let go!"

To my surprise, she did. "Stupid girl!" she said. "Just because he doesn't look like your precious Icarus! Icarus looks like a girl."

Outraged, I opened my mouth to protest, but she rushed on.

"But that doesn't matter. What matters is that I bear Theseus's child."

"*What!* What do you mean? You couldn't possibly —"

"I do! I know I do! I can feel it, here." She sank down onto the bed and caressed the region of her stomach.

"But —" I might not have known everything there was to know on this subject, but I was quite certain that a baby didn't simply appear in a woman's womb because she wished it. "You've barely even spoken to the man!"

She looked away. A smile tugged at the corners of her lips.

"Oh, I have done more than that," she said.

"Ariadne! You haven't! You found him then?"

"Yes. Icarus was right. Theseus *was* under the Bull Court. I followed the servant to his very cell. It was so dark and drear, Xenodice! I was frightened. I could feel the ancient dead pressing up against me, whispering in my ear." She shuddered. "But then I found him. How glad he was to see me!"

"Well, yes, he would be," I said. Fighting a sense of dread at the pit of my stomach, I asked, "Is he then at liberty?"

"No," she said. "I told you he wasn't!"

"Then how —?"

"Oh, I got into his cell easily enough. It wasn't even guarded. But one of his arms is manacled to the wall and I have no means to free him. Daedalus holds the only key. Xenodice, you must help me! Our mother will kill him as soon as Acalle returns, and that is at any moment!"

"Acalle! Returning? What do you mean?"

"What I said, of course."

"She is not dead then? Or — I thought perhaps she was under an enchantment. Was that why she did not come home for so long?"

"Oh, you are so stupid, Xenodice! Of course she wasn't! She was only pregnant by the King of Libya. She went away to have the baby, and now that it is born, and thankfully not a girl, she is coming home again."

"Pregnant! But — wait! Why should she not have a girl child? I would like to have a little niece."

"I could shake you, Xenodice, really I could," she said, and did so. "Listen! If the baby was a girl, she might someday try to claim the throne, even though she was illegitimate and the product of an inferior alliance. As Acalle's firstborn she could cause problems for Acalle's first *legitimate* daughter. You see? So a girl baby would have to be exposed on the rocks to die as soon as it was born. But as it happens, it was a boy. Acalle has only been waiting until he was old enough to be handed over to a wet nurse to raise, and now she is returning."

"Oh!" I said. "I see." I sat down on the bed beside her. "But why couldn't we be told?"

"Because even the rumor of such a child could someday stir up trouble, that's why. Apparently absolutely *everybody* has known all along that Acalle wasn't dead or gone for good, that she was just off studying with some famous holy woman in the Eastern Isles. No one spoke of it because it was supposed to be some big, secret, religious experience. What only Mother knew was that Acalle was pregnant when she left. But no one" — Ariadne's face was white and set — "no one thought to tell *me* anything about anything."

"Oh, Ariadne," I said. "I am sorry."

"Never mind. I was furious when Mother first told me, but now I'm *glad*, because I'm going to leave here with Theseus."

"What?" I cried.

"And why not?" she demanded. "Do you suppose I want to stay here with no husband and an illegitimate child and have Acalle made queen over my head?"

"But perhaps you are not pregnant after all. You might be mistaken."

"I am not mistaken! I tell you, I know it!"

"All right! All right! Perhaps you are right. But you couldn't want to leave Kefti and go to Athens!"

"I could! I do! At least I would be queen there."

"If Theseus married you, you mean. But you would not be queen of Athens in the same way that Acalle will be queen of Kefti. They do not honor women there as we do here on Kefti."

"What do you mean, *if* Theseus married me? Of course he will marry me. He loves me. He says he cannot live without me!"

"That much is certainly true," I said.

"Xenodice, how cynical you've become! Let me tell you, it's very unbecoming in a young girl. If you must know, *I* cannot live without *him*. And anyway," she added, more prosaically, "he couldn't possibly hope for a better match than Princess Ariadne of the Isle of Kefti."

"Ye-es," I agreed.

Ariadne's nostrils flared and her eyes narrowed. "Why do you say 'yes' like that? Do you suggest that I, *I!* am not worthy to wed the future king of *Athens*? How dare you, Xenodice!"

"Oh, yes, of course." I hurried to appease her. "You would be a very great prize indeed if you wedded with our mother's consent, but as it is —"

"Theseus considers me a great prize with or without our mother's consent," Ariadne said coldly.

"Even if — even if your flight leads to warfare between Athens and Kefti?" I asked, trembling before her anger.

"Yes! Yes! Even then."

"Oh, my sister, I fear for you!" I said. Knowing it would have been better to remain silent but unable to help myself, I added, "And on top of everything else he is so *very* unattractive!"

"He is not! Stop *saying* that, Xenodice!"

"But I do not understand! Why would you wish to tie yourself to a slave, and one condemned by our mother to die? It makes no sense."

She hesitated. I could see that she did not believe me capable of sympathizing but desperately needed to talk about her lover to someone.

"He is a hero, Xenodice," she said very seriously. "He is the greatest hero of our time."

"Yes," I agreed, "so he told us."

"Oh, you are like everyone else! We are too civilized

here on Kefti. Our island has been tamed for a thousand years. There is no wilderness here — the Queen's Menagerie holds the only dangerous beasts of prey. What need have we for heroes? Theseus comes from a primitive world, where heroes matter. He is rough and wild because the world he comes from is rough and wild. He wasn't boasting when he called himself a hero — he was just stating a fact."

"It sounded like boasting," I said. "And that's all the more reason not to leave Kefti for Athens. Who knows what would happen to you there!"

She smiled a secret smile, hugging herself. "Theseus will protect me," she said. "He will never let any harm come to me. Do you know what he did?" she demanded. "He is — everyone has guessed that he is illegitimate, but he is the son of a princess, not some milkmaid or woodcutter's daughter. His mother is the daughter of King Pittheus of Troezen."

"Oh, really?" Troezen was a tiny coastal nation across the sea, of no importance to anyone but its inhabitants.

"When he reached manhood he *walked* from Troezen to Athens to claim his patrimony, although his mother begged him to sail. The lands between Troezen and Athens were infested with all manner of monsters and thieves and murderers, but he *would not* take the easy way, because he wished to prove himself a hero."

"And did he meet any monsters or murderers on his way to Athens?" I inquired.

"He did. He killed them all," she said. "There were scores and scores of them! There was Sinis, for example. He used to tie people to two pine trees bent to the ground. Then he'd let the trees go and the people would fly through the air into the sea. It must have been a sight to see," she mused. "Theseus served Sinis in exactly the same manner.

"And then — listen, Xenodice! — this is very strange. The robber Procrustes owned an iron bed, and when strangers passed through his lands he would force them to lie on it. If you were too tall to fit the frame you had your feet cut off, and if you were too short you'd be *stretched* so you were long enough!"

"Ugh!" I said involuntarily. What queer savages these mainlanders were!

"And then he met one Sciron, a bandit who —"

"Why?" I asked.

"Why what?" Ariadne demanded.

"Why did Procrustes do that, stretching people and chopping them up? Why should he care?"

"Oh, I don't know. He was just mean. Anyway, Theseus bound Procrustes to his own bed, killed him, and left him there for the crows and birds of prey," she concluded with satisfaction. "After that there were lots more he vanquished, like a fierce sow and a wrestler who broke people's necks and I don't know what all else. And then when he got to Athens, everybody was naturally shouting out his praises in the streets, since he had made that whole part of the world safe. He was so popular, in fact, that his father — who didn't know he was his father, you understand — got worried. Not having an heir, he didn't much like bold young men who might be tempted to take the country away from him. So he invited Theseus to dinner with the idea of poisoning him."

I gasped. "*Another* violation of the sacred law of hospitality! Truly this Aegeus is a barbarian!"

"Well, it wasn't actually his idea," Ariadne said. "There was at court a witch named Medea, who knew by her arts who Theseus was and who wanted no rivals for the love of the king. So she convinced Aegeus to give his son a cup of poisoned wine."

"Still —"

"But Medea's plot failed," Ariadne said rapidly, "because just as Theseus was about to drink, his father saw the sword he carried and the sandals he wore, by which he knew the boy was his son. He dashed the cup from Theseus's lips and pressed him to his bosom, whereupon the witch Medea stole away and fled from that court and was never seen there again."

"Hmmmm," I said. "What, then, is he doing here in a consignment of slaves?"

"That is the bravest thing he has done so far," she said eagerly. "He volunteered to come here. He thinks — they all think in Athens — that the Minotaur —"

"Do not call him that!" I said. "His name is Asterius, and he is our brother."

Rather than firing up at my peremptory tone, she did not meet my eyes. "Yes," she said, and then went on. "They believe that he eats Athenians. I *told* Theseus that he did not — really, I did, Xenodice. But once Theseus gets an idea in his head, well, it's remarkably difficult to get it out."

"A pleasant trait in a husband," I observed.

"Oh, what do you know about the matter?" she said furiously. "No more than Molus, or that baby Phaedra! He is the only husband I shall ever have, so hold your tongue!"

I was about to reply, when I thought better of it. I knew what it was to be bound to a man by fate. I would marry Icarus or I would marry no one. And then too, the mainland sounded like a terrible place, lawless and wild — it was no place for me. But Ariadne had a brave, bold heart, just as Theseus had. Perhaps she belonged there, as she would not belong on Kefti now that Acalle was coming home.

Ariadne was watching me.

"Help me, Xenodice."

"No! How can I? He will hurt Asterius — I know he

will! He frightens me, Ariadne. There is another matter —" I broke off, unwilling to betray my father. I didn't know how Ariadne would use such knowledge.

"He won't! I promise you, he won't harm Asterius. I will make him swear!"

If Theseus could be bound by a promise not to harm my brother, why then . . . he could be sent away before my father found him, before my father managed somehow to release him. Before he pressed a knife into his hand and led him to my brother's quarters . . . My mind worked furiously. More than anything, I wanted him gone from the Labyrinth. And, though I did not much like Theseus, I was entirely willing to see him depart for Athens rather than for the Underworld.

"But you will need a ship, provisioned, and oarsmen, too! What can *I* do in such a hopeless case?"

"Get me the key, Xenodice," she said.

Was it only a few weeks ago that she sent me into the orchard to steal figs? Now, with the same assurance of my obedience, I was being sent to commit a treasonous act against my mother, my queen, and my country.

"But I may be caught!" I objected.

"That," said Ariadne, "is why I want *you* to do it."

"Oh, but Ariadne!"

CHAPTER TEN

In the Workshop

"I ONLY MEANT THAT DAEDALUS AND ICARUS ARE BOTH FOND of you, so if you *are* caught, they won't tell our mother. Nobody notices what you do anyway. You're always loitering around Daedalus's workshop, talking to Icarus."

"I am not!" I protested.

"Xenodice, listen. The servants still think of me as the heir, so they watch me day and night. If I tried to steal the key, I'd be caught. In fact," she said, looking apprehensively toward the door, "it won't be long before they come looking for me."

"I thought you said that everybody already knew about Acalle," I said.

"Oh, you know what I meant. The important people knew. Not the servants."

She sounded impatient. Evidently believing that she had gained her point, she now wanted to move on to other matters. I, however, was not giving up so easily.

"It seems to me," I argued, "that someone clever enough

to get herself pregnant without the knowledge of vigilant watchers could certainly manage to steal a key."

"That's the problem," she said. "They're getting suspicious." She got up, moved to the door, and peered out into the hallway. Satisfied, she came back and stood by the bed. "I nearly had to force wine down the throat of that stupid Salamis just now to keep her from following me."

Salamis was the slave girl who waited on my sister.

"You got her drunk? How could you —?" I stared, aghast, imagining my sister forcibly pouring enough wine into Salamis to render her incapable.

"It was drugged, of course," Ariadne said impatiently. "How else do you think I've been getting away? Ever since she caught me coming back to bed at dawn she simply will *not* leave me alone. I've been putting poppy juice in her wine every evening for weeks. Only, after a while it doesn't seem to work as well."

"No, I suppose not," I said.

"You stay here for a bit after I leave," she directed. "If they guess that I have gone to the trouble to drug Salamis in order to talk to you in private, they'll start watching *you*, and that will ruin our plans."

I followed her unhappily to the door. As she entered the hallway she paused and turned to look at me.

"Not a word to anyone, do you hear? If you open your

mouth it will be your undoing, as well as mine and Theseus's."

She had gripped my injured wrist again, but I did not protest this time. The hall was shadowy; the lamps were unlit at this time of day. Her face looked different — older and haggard. I was seized with a sudden terror, not for myself but for her.

"Oh, Ariadne, are you entirely certain that you are doing the right thing? Reconsider, I beg of you!" I cried.

Was there ever anyone in the history of the world who changed a cherished course of action upon hearing such a plea? No one with Ariadne's mind and spirit, at any rate.

"Don't be such a goose." To my amazement, she put her arm around me and kissed my cheek. "Oh, Xenodice, we are going to be so happy! He has promised to teach me how to interpret the winds, and he's going to whittle me a reed pipe and show me how to play music on it. He knows everything; he can do everything! And he says" — her eyes softened — "he'll give me a bear cub for my own, when next he kills a nursing mother."

What a descent was this! Ariadne, whose chariot had so lately been drawn by winged cheetahs! Ariadne, proud daughter of a nation so rich in wisdom, the land of magicians, healers, and seers! To be dazzled by the promised gift of a bear cub and the tricks of any sailor or shepherd! It broke my heart.

Still, I could see that there was no persuading her, and I found myself much moved by her kiss and caress. I sighed and uttered promises of discretion.

"Do it quickly, Xenodice!" she said, releasing me. "Every moment that passes brings Acalle closer, and the day my mother regains her heir, Aegeus will lose his. I know it," she said in response to my questioning glance, "because she told me so. That's why she hasn't had him put to death yet. It's symbolic or something — I don't know. But Acalle will be back soon, and then . . . Oh, Xenodice, you must hurry! Remember: the day of Theseus's death will be the day of mine also."

I frowned as she walked away. Did she love him so much that she would make an end to herself if she lost him?

If Icarus were to sink into the Underworld, I asked myself, would I seek to follow him? Perhaps — I could not say. But that was quite a different matter. My life had been intertwined with Icarus's for so long that if I were suddenly torn from him it would be like losing a limb. Ariadne had known this man for only a few short weeks. Still, she had lain with him and believed herself to bear his child. That must make a difference.

Musing on these matters, I slowly made my way downstairs. I was trying to avoid thinking about a more pressing concern — how I was to obtain possession of the key. For, somehow, it had been agreed on between us that I would do this thing for Ariadne.

One thing I had determined without pausing for consideration was that *if* I obtained possession of the key and *if* Ariadne managed to arrange a means of escape from Kefti, I would insist on personally seeing Theseus conducted out of the Labyrinth. I did not know whether or not I could trust my sister with Asterius's life; I knew I could *not* trust Theseus.

I wished more than anything to be able to put the matter away from me, to forget it for a little while at least. But I knew that when Ariadne had determined something she was like a dog on a rat. I would not be released until either one of two things occurred: she held the key in her hand, or Theseus was dead.

I considered the problem. Where might Daedalus have hidden the key? What if he kept it on his person? But no, I did not think he would go so far. He would not expect that anyone would wish to free Theseus other than the Athenian slaves, and they had not the freedom to wander about the maze searching for him.

He would keep the key somewhere concealed but close by, where he might lay his hand upon it quickly when so directed by the queen. I did not think that the place of concealment would be in their bedroom, where he spent so little time. Rather, it would be in the big, untidy room where he and Icarus labored every day.

I was glad to feel freed of the necessity of searching the bedroom. At the thought of being discovered there, handling his and Icarus's private possessions, a wave of humiliation dyed my cheeks red. It would be bad enough looking through the workshop.

I hastened there, however, wishing to complete a task so distasteful as quickly as possible. To my relief, no one was there. The fire was out, and no signs of ongoing activity warned of their imminent return. Daedalus and Icarus were perhaps looking over the site where a new fountain was to be erected in the western courtyard. I uttered a swift prayer of thanksgiving to the Goddess and began my search.

As usual, the room looked as though it had been ransacked. Heaps of objects were scattered all over the floor, the long table, and one of the windowsills. Prepared paints, discarded brushes, knives, and carving tools. Lengths of wood, broken shards of pottery, odd scraps of cloth. Metal fasteners, three saws of varying sizes, a pair of tongs, a long-handled razor, and six tweezers laid out in order of length. A pile of animal hides, stiffened with age. The remains of three meals, furred over with mold. Several pottery mugs with the dregs of old wine lingering in the bottoms. Stacks of clay tablets with diagrams hastily sketched on their leathery surfaces. A bowl containing olive pits, a metal toothpick, and a large seal stone depicting a lion with his paw on a dove.

After I had made one complete circuit of the room, carefully picking up and replacing each item I encountered, I sank down onto a mound of overstuffed sacks on the floor, discouraged. How anyone could find anything in this chaos I could not imagine. Nor did it seem possible that objects of great beauty rose out of this trash pit on a regular basis.

Truth to tell, I did not even know precisely what I was searching for. Locks and keys are rare; secrecy is thought to give greater security than a mere mechanical device for protecting items of value. I had therefore only the haziest idea of what a key might look like. It ought to be small, I thought, smaller than my hand, and made of wood or metal.

I began to pick through the pile of clay tablets for want of anything better to do. I did not believe that I would find the key under them, but if anyone came in this would seem a reasonable, though prying and officious, activity for me to be engaged in. Besides, it gave me a chance to think.

Most of the tablets were boring — engineering calculations and architectural designs — but some were rather amusing, and I became distracted from the question of where the key might be hidden. I recognized several as being executed by Icarus, who had marked them with a tiny sketch of a falcon in the lower corner. I pored over these for some time, tracing with my finger the lines scratched in clay, which represented a hunting cat bent over a pool of fish — a design for a jewelry box, perhaps.

Something inside the sack on which I sat was pricking my bottom — several somethings, in fact. Upon investigation I found that the sack, as well as the three sacks underneath that, contained large quantities of feathers. *Feathers?*

I shifted the pile of tablets again, looking for a particular one. Yes, here it was, a man with wings. He was shown in front and back view, and to the side was drawn a framework partially covered with layers of overlapping feathers.

I stared incredulously from the tablet to the sacks and sacks of pigeon feathers. My eye traveled farther and found leaning against the wall a wooden frame exactly like the one in the picture, except that it had no feathers on it. Had Daedalus gone mad?

"I see you have discovered my hiding place, Princess," said a voice close to my ear.

I shrieked.

Daedalus stood before me, his head cocked to one side.

"W-what?" I stammered. "Hiding place?"

He said nothing, just stood looking at me. I looked down and found that my investigation of the feather sacks had uncovered a dark, wedge-shaped crack in the floor. One of the stones that made up the floor had been removed and then improperly replaced before being covered up with feather sacks. Stooping over, I pried the heavy block farther out of its usual position so that light fell on the cavity below.

It was a safe, of course. There were jewelry and weapons safes all over the Labyrinth. As Daedalus had supervised the construction of his workshop, it was hardly surprising that he had made sure to install one for himself. I ought to have thought of it before. On the other hand, it was lucky I had not, as this would have necessitated a tedious interlude, crawling around on my hands and knees feeling the edges of the floor stones.

Then, inside the safe, I saw the key lying in a golden cup. I recognized it for what it was at once and picked it up.

"The key to the manacles binding Prince Theseus, my lady," Daedalus informed me.

"Yes, I know," I said. "Daedalus, are you planning to fly like a bird?"

He raised his eyebrows at the change of subject. "I had thought of it, perhaps," he admitted.

"There are sacks of feathers here," I observed, "and a frame for a set of wings all completed."

"Since you press me, my lady, it has been a lifetime dream for me, and I believe I am close to achieving it."

"But is there any chance that such a scheme could succeed?"

Seeing my interest, he began to warm to the subject.

"I believe so, my lady. I have made many attempts at flight before, all unsuccessful. But this time I think it will work."

I picked up the wing structure and turned it over in my hands. "How do you attach the feathers?" I asked.

"The larger pinions are tied on, and the smaller feathers attached with a glue I have made from pine pitch and beeswax," he said.

"I would like to fly. But would it be safe?"

"Nothing in life is safe, Princess. Certainly not flying."

"I am not a brave person," I said, and sighed. "At any rate, I would like to see someone else fly up into the sky."

"Then I hope that you shall, Princess." He smiled at me. "And now, tell me if you will, what you plan to do with that key."

There seemed little point in concealment now. "Ariadne wishes to free Theseus and flee with him to Athens," I said.

"I see. And how do you come into this plot?"

"I want him to go far away and not come back. He frightens me," I said, sounding like a little girl.

"For your brother's sake?"

I nodded.

He was silent for a long moment, thinking. "Perhaps you are wise," he said at last. "Your father has been trying to bribe me to tell him where Theseus is being held. He doesn't like to speak too plainly — it's dangerous for him if his reason for wanting to know is what I think it is — but it's clear enough what he wants. I have so far pretended not to understand him, but I cannot hold off telling him much longer."

"Oh, do not tell him!"

Daedalus eyed me speculatively. "I thought at first he wished to know so that he could kill Theseus himself. He has as much reason to hate him as your mother has. But Androgeus died long ago. I am beginning to think —"

"He wants Theseus to kill my brother," I burst out. "He hates the Lord Asterius."

Daedalus nodded. "That was my idea also," he said. He sat in thought for a moment. "I will help you."

I gaped at him. "You will? Why?"

Then I remembered. Theseus was some sort of relation, Icarus had said. Suddenly it occurred to me that Daedalus and Icarus would be in terrible danger if Theseus escaped. It would seem that Daedalus had deliberately let him go.

"No," I said. I knelt down and put the key back into the golden cup in the safe and began to rock the stone back and forth, easing it back into place. "No, Daedalus."

What a fool I was! I ought to have never listened to Ariadne. Every path led to death; if Theseus did not die, why then Daedalus and Icarus very well might. Let it be Theseus, then; Ariadne would forget about him in time.

I pulled the heavy sacks of feathers back over the floor safe and arranged them to look natural. "It is too dangerous, Daedalus," I said. "They would know it was you who freed him. You must not take such risks."

"Very well, Princess," he said, and I could not read the expression on his face.

I paused in the doorway. "Do you think —?"

"Yes, Princess?"

"Do you think that I might learn to fly someday?"

"Would you not be afraid?"

"Yes, I would. But to fly like a bird, Daedalus! That would be wonderful."

"Yes," he agreed.

"And although I am a princess, I am not an important one. If I died it would not be a serious problem."

He smiled and shook his head. "You are still a princess. If anything should happen to your older sisters, you will be queen."

"I would much rather fly than be queen," I said.

"I am sorry. But I promise that you shall be the first to see a man fly. The first in the world."

"Well, thank you for that, at least," I said sadly.

"You are welcome, my princess." And he bowed deeply, rapping his forehead sharply with his knuckles.

I had been wrong to leave the Bull Pen even for a few hours. That was the only way to keep my brother safe. My father surely would not seek to have my brother slain if he knew that I never left his side. From now on I would eat and sleep in the Bull Pen. I stopped by my rooms to inform my servant, Maira, of my decision. She protested, but I was firm.

"See to it," I said, and hurried back to my brother, fearful that my father had somehow managed to free Theseus while I dallied in the workshop.

I ordered the Athenians to withdraw during the night to a small room down the hall from the Bull Pen. I would have liked to dismiss them altogether, but that was beyond my powers. I wanted an armed soldier to stand guard over my brother's slumbers, but the soldiers were my father's men and loyal to him. In the end, Maira slept on the floor by my couch while a manservant kept watch by the door.

It appeared that my brother was far from an ideal roommate. I could almost feel that his servants were ill used after all. I soon understood the gratitude with which they greeted my news that they would not be sleeping in the same chamber with him any longer. His snoring was prodigious. One might be excused for thinking his sleeping place the cave of some bloodstained, man-eating monster, with such terrible roars and whistles issuing out of it every night. I pulled the bedclothes down around my ears and snatched such sleep as I might.

In the morning, the captain of my father's guards, Rhesos, appeared and informed me that the king wished to know why I had chosen to take up residence in my brother's chambers.

"Tell my father," I said, "that the Lady Potnia appeared to me in a dream and told me that there is a grave danger to the life of Lord Asterius, and that my presence alone would keep him safe."

This was not strictly true, of course, but I felt certain that the Goddess would forgive me, as it was surely through her intervention that I had learned about my father's plot.

Rhesos looked as though he would speak further, but then seemed to think better of it. "Yes, my lady," he said, and left me.

How my father received this reply I do not know, for Rhesos did not return to demand further particulars of this menace to my brother's life, and neither did my father.

CHAPTER ELEVEN

A Clew of Thread

AND SO I SIT AND STILL I SPIN. MY CLEW OF THREAD GROWS long and longer.

I am so tired of spinning! Yet I seem compelled to spin as long as my weary wrists can hold up my work.

There are no windows here, only the light well, open to the sky. I can watch the clouds go by, but I must bend my neck backward to an uncomfortable angle, and so even this source of entertainment palls after a short time.

I am a prisoner in the Bull Pen; it is my own doing, but I am a prisoner all the same. I do not enjoy anticipating the death of a fellow human being. I wish that it were otherwise — I wish that Theseus could leave this island unharmed. But sometimes I feel that I would willingly see a thousand Theseuses walk to their deaths if it meant that I could once again sleep in my own quiet bed.

I dread the moment when Ariadne comes to demand the key. That she has not already done so is strange. Perhaps she is so busy with other arrangements for their escape that she has no leisure to badger me. I am sorry she is being put to so much trouble for nothing, but at least it keeps her occupied and away from me.

My greatest happiness now is my brother's. He does not understand why I am spending so much time with him, but he is delighted. He frisks like a young calf in the springtime. He brings me such treasures as he has hidden away in the straw: a gray stone with a round hole in it, a rusty metal bolt, a raven's feather. Often he lies down beside me and rests his horned head in my lap. Then I cease from spinning for a time to comb his hair and sing him nonsense songs.

Acalle is home; Maira told me so. Maira was nearly out of her head with excitement at the news. I merely went on twisting flax into thread, spinning my worries into a fine white linen strand.

"Yes, of course," I said to Maira.

I was not as pleased as I had expected to be.

"Then you knew where she was?" Maira asked, surprised.

I shrugged. It seemed of little importance now.

I thought of Ariadne, and how she must have felt when she heard. I thought of Theseus, pent up in his stone prison beneath the Bull Court.

I was right — I was *right* to do nothing. Theseus deserved to die — certainly he deserved it more than Asterius, or Daedalus and Icarus. Theseus was only a slave, anyway.

When would they come for him, I wondered, tonight or tomorrow?

Meanwhile, I refused to stir from my brother's side. My mother sent to see why I did not come to greet my sister, and I returned the same answer I had given my father.

Tomorrow night there would be a great feast to celebrate Acalle's arrival. Mother would surely insist upon my attendance, but I could not leave Asterius until assured that Theseus was dead. There would be little joy in such a festivity for me. I would be glad to see Acalle, but we had never been close. As prickly and difficult as Ariadne sometimes was, I could not imagine my life without her. If she were to leave with Theseus there would be a large hole in my life. But I would lose her anyway; Ariadne would not lightly forgive.

The sky above the light well had grown dark, my evening meal was consumed, and still Ariadne had not come. I ought to have been grateful, but it made me uneasy. Maira lit a single lamp — it was dangerous to burn more than one in this room full of hay and straw — and began to play the lyre.

I sang. I do not have a beautiful singing voice. Rather the reverse, in fact, but Maira knew better than to point this out, and singing eased my anxiety. Asterius made some peculiar noises in his throat, which might have been interpreted as an attempt to participate in the music, and in this way we passed the long evening.

At length we prepared for sleep. I instructed Maira and the manservant who guarded the door to move my bed as close as possible to where Asterius slept and resigned myself to a restless night. In fact, I fell asleep almost at once.

I could not tell what it was at first that awakened me. Asterius, for a wonder, was silent. An absolute stillness seemed to have fallen over the Labyrinth. The lamp was out, and I could scarcely see my hand held up before my face.

As I lay there, wondering why I was awake, I heard it again: a soft, stealthy bumping against the leg of the couch I slept on. I peered over the edge but could see nothing. I disliked feeling for the source of the noise. It might so easily be a rat — but it didn't sound quite like an animal. Finally, hesitantly, I ran my hand down the side of the bed. Just above the floor I encountered something I did not understand: a fine wire or string, tautly stretched.

It moved under my fingers.

I snatched my hand back. For a moment I lay motionless, utterly perplexed. Then I understood. The great ball of linen thread I had spun lay on the floor. The end of that thread passed through a narrow gap between the bed and a heavy grain bin. The noise I heard was the clew of thread slowly unraveling, rolling this way and that, trapped behind the bed and the grain bin.

I leapt out of bed. My foot struck Maira where she lay sleeping on the floor.

"Get up!" I whispered harshly, bending down to shake the girl by the shoulder. "Get up *now!*"

She did not respond. I slapped her face and she mumbled faintly, then subsided into sleep again.

Terrified, I hurried to my brother's side. He lay as still and unresponsive as Maira, but my groping fingers could find no wound. He still breathed. I disturbed his slumber only enough so that he twisted into another position and began to snore.

Already guessing what I would find, I crept over to the doorway and found the servant who was supposed to be keeping watch slumped over, deep in sleep.

The wine. Maira and the servant had had at least two glasses each, while I had only tasted mine, not liking the flavor. Asterius did not drink wine, but perhaps — yes, it could have been concealed in the little grain cake prepared especially for him.

I thought of Ariadne drugging her servant's wine. Now

I knew why she had not come to demand the key. In some way she had learned that I did not have it, that I had decided not to help. And now —

There was a faint noise here in the doorway, barely perceptible over Asterius's snores. I bent down, feeling along the opening.

The thread stretched from my bedside out through the door. The noise I had heard was the slight scraping of thread against stone. Ariadne had entered the Bull Pen while we slept, picked up the end of the thread, and walked away holding it, the ball unwinding behind.

Why? That I could guess easily enough. She would descend to Theseus's cell and give him the free end. Then, while she crept out to the harbor to secure the ship and supplies she must have waiting there, Theseus would be able to find his way to the Bull Pen.

I was furious. Perhaps I did not think as clearly as I should have, but I was too angry to think, to ask myself the motive for doing such a thing.

It was reasonable that Ariadne would wish to free her lover, even that she would wish to escape with him. But the only reason for the clew of thread that occurred to me was to allow Theseus to travel in the dark, through unknown passageways, to where my brother and his protectors lay in a drugged sleep.

Oh, it was cruel, it was hard! Any regret I felt for leaving Theseus to his fate and any affection I felt for Ariadne dropped away from me now. Why should she revenge herself on Asterius? I could understand and accept anger directed at me, but of all the actors in this tragedy, Asterius at least was wholly innocent.

I thought for a brief moment of feeling around in the dark until I found the lamp. There might be hot coals in a fire pit somewhere along the way, and light would be most welcome. But I dared not spare the time. I didn't know how close Ariadne was to reaching Theseus or whether or not she had possession of the key.

After all, what did the darkness matter to me? I too had the clew of thread for a guide. I circled my index finger and thumb around it and walked forward, letting it slide unhindered through my fingers. I had no desire to signal to Ariadne that someone else walked the Labyrinth behind her.

I soon adjusted my pace so that it matched hers; the thread lay unmoving in my hand. At first I traveled well-known territory; even in the blackness I knew where I was. Soon, however, I descended a staircase I did not recognize, and then another, plunging deeper into the earth than I had ever known that the maze descended. At last I walked down a hall so narrow my shoulders nearly brushed the wall on each side. The floors under my naked feet were earthen, not stone, and crumbs of broken masonry underfoot made my progress painful and uncertain.

I remembered what Ariadne had said about how she could sense the ancient dead there underneath the Labyrinth, and the hairs stood up on the nape of my neck. It was true; I also felt them, I also heard them. Surely, for instance, there was something looming off to the side just ahead. I could see nothing, but I paused, so certain was I that something waited there in the pitchy black.

Yet while I stood motionless, Ariadne walked closer and closer to the enemy. I sighed and stepped forward.

Powerful arms wrapped around me and a hand clamped over my mouth before I could scream. In my shock I dropped the thread and was dragged roughly through an opening into what I dimly sensed was a small room, a cell, perhaps, like the one that imprisoned Theseus. Something hard and sharp pressed against my neck.

"Who goes there?" demanded a hoarse whisper. "Speak and identify yourself or I'll cut your throat."

The hand over my mouth loosened slightly.

I swallowed, trying to conquer a quaver of terror.

"It is —"

"Keep your voice down!" commanded the man. "Whisper!"

I lowered my voice, but not by much. "It is I, Princess Xenodice of Knossos, daughter of Queen Pasiphae. I descend in an uninterrupted line from the Goddess Potnia, whose dwelling place and temple this is," I said. "If you do me any harm whatsoever, you will suffer greatly."

"Pah!" There was someone else in the room, and that someone did not like my answer.

Nor did the man who held me.

"I swear they slept," he said, and I thought that he addressed not me but the other person. "They should all of them have slept like the dead." He turned his attention back to me. "You shall not be hurt, Princess, unless you speak. If you make one more sound, you will die."

I went still. I had thought that it was Theseus who had captured me, but now I was not sure. Who, then, was the second person? Ariadne? No, there was no point in bringing him the clew of thread if she then remained to guide him. She would be waiting in the ship until he joined her with his comrades.

Besides, intuition told me it was a man. It seemed to me that the man in the corner commanded and the man with the knife obeyed.

I felt cold bronze on my throat. The knife had been turned so that the flat lay against my skin.

"Sssh," came a warning from the darkness.

I too waited, listening. Footsteps in the hallway approached the chamber in which we stood. They passed, and continued on in the direction whence I had come. We waited, then followed after.

It had been a long journey down into the earth. Returning to the Bull Pen with a knife to my throat seemed a voyage without an end. I was forced to walk crammed up against this strange man, who clutched my arm with one hand and the knife with the other. I could smell his nervous sweat, hear his ragged breath in my ear. If he was Theseus, he was at least as frightened as I was.

The other man walked noiselessly behind us.

Gradually, the halls through which we passed lost their absolute darkness and tomblike chill. The prevailing odor became less earthy; I smelled lamp oil and last night's dinner. The floors were smooth and cool under my bruised feet. I began to believe that I knew where I was.

The knife was still pressed into my flesh. It had not slipped or faltered in our long walk. If I cried out, if I tried to pull away, it could be turned on me in an instant. We were approaching the Bull Pen now, I was certain — the scent of hay and straw now intermingled with the other odors. I did not know what I was going to do.

I began to hear the rumbling, reverberating snores of my brother, so like the growls of a wild animal in its den.

I saw a light ahead, one that flickered and wavered as though carried in the hand of someone walking ahead of us. We were overtaking the person whose footsteps had passed our door in the deep maze. Suddenly the man who held me stopped. His hand came up and covered my mouth again. Other hands came and took me from him. After a moment of confusion, I realized that I was now held prisoner by the man who had followed us through the darkness.

The little scuffle occasioned by this transfer alerted the one who held the lamp. The light ahead of us paused, remained stationary in the entrance to the Bull Pen.

"Theseus!" The cry came from the man ahead, the one who had held me until a moment ago. No longer hushed, his voice rang out clearly. "A gift from the gods of your fathers!"

There came a clang and a clatter, as something metallic hit the floor and skittered down the hall toward the light. Now I could dimly see that a man held the lamp. He hesitated, then bent and picked the object up, examining it in the lamplight.

It was the knife.

Under the smothering hand I opened my jaws wide and bit down as hard as I could. The hand dropped, the man who held me uttered a smothered oath, and I screamed.

"No!"

I fought like a mad creature. Why had I not realized before that the knife no longer menaced my throat?

I sought to do as much damage as I could. I drew my knee up and kicked savagely backward at the man's groin. My elbows pummeled his gut, and when I was able to twist a little sideways my fingernails searched for his face and eyes.

For one brief moment, I thought that I could fight free. The ferocity of my attack had taken my opponent by surprise, and I knew I had hurt him: he groaned and cursed in a most satisfying manner. But almost immediately the other man, the one who had forcibly escorted me up from the deep maze, came to his assistance. I kicked and bit, but to no avail. After a few agonizing moments, we three ended up in a heap on the floor, with myself undermost.

I could not move. The combined weight of two adult men nearly crushed the life out of me. We lay there, panting.

It was in this humiliating and helpless position that I heard my brother's death cries.

They seemed to go on and on, small sounds, not loud. First a thud and then a smothered cry, over and over again. A final thud and then a sigh. Later I learned that, not content with killing my brother as he lay in a drugged sleep, Theseus had murdered Maira and the guard as well.

If I had been there he would have murdered me, too.

When the killings were over and silence had fallen, the two men who had armed Theseus dragged me, unresisting, away. Behind, I heard many feet running toward the Bull Pen.

CHAPTER TWELVE

My World Unmade

TWO OF MY BROTHERS STILL LIVE: THE YOUNGEST, GLAUCUS AND Molus. The others, Androgeus, Deucalion, Catreus, and Asterius, have fallen to Aegeus or to his son, Theseus. My sister Ariadne is gone, fled with Theseus. Icarus and Daedalus are imprisoned. My mother lies paralyzed in her bed, felled by a seizure that has deprived her of speech and movement. And my father's face bears the marks of my fingernails.

Which of these matters ought I to grieve over first? I cannot tell.

This is how it came to take place.

That night after I was dragged away, the Athenians — those who had arrived with Theseus — rallied to their prince. It was their footsteps I had heard running toward the Bull Pen. They fled from the Labyrinth down to the sea, where Ariadne waited with a ship.

Did Ariadne weep to see her brother's blood staining her lover's hands? I do not know, for I never again saw her among the living. Reflecting on these events in later days, I came to believe that she never intended to lead Theseus to Asterius, but simply to guide him, unarmed, to the place where his compatriots slept. Whatever tale Theseus might choose to tell in Athens, it was my father's gift of the knife that led to the murders, not the clew of thread. Or so I think.

It had no doubt been their hope to steal away in silence, but my screams aroused my brothers Deucalion and Catreus. Not finding my father in his bed, they pursued the Athenians alone, not even pausing to collect a company of soldiers to aid them.

I was not present at the skirmish on the quay, and for that I am thankful. Ariadne may have been innocent in the death of her brother Asterius, but she could not be held blameless in the deaths of Catreus and Deucalion. That ship was fully armed, and Ariadne must have procured the sword that cleaved Catreus from throat to hip and the knife that plunged into Deucalion's heart. Deucalion had not even had time to snatch up a weapon; the Athenians killed an unarmed man.

I myself was thrust half fainting into an empty chamber and there abandoned by my abductors. I did not pursue them; I had not the heart. Fool that I was, I thought that the worst had happened, that no further evil could touch us. I sank down on the floor and remained there, dully weeping, until the sun rose and a maidservant found me. Upon seeing my prostrate body she began to scream.

"Dead! Dead! I have found the Princess Xenodice, and she too is dead!"

"Oh, be quiet!" I said, sitting up. "I'm nothing of the sort."

This further unnerved the girl, who shrieked without cessation until Graia arrived and slapped her soundly across the face.

No one had noticed my absence at first in all the confusion, but when Asterius, Maira, and the manservant were discovered dead, they began to search for me. Strangely, they thought that it was I who had departed with Theseus. It was believed that he had taken me as a hostage in his flight. No one thought to question Ariadne's whereabouts until I asked for her, and only then did it become clear that she and a great quantity of her jewelry, clothing, and other personal possessions were missing.

My mother withstood the blows of that dreadful dawn with remarkable fortitude, or so it appeared at first. The night before, she had retired to bed with nine children under her roof — one restored to her only that day. Before the sun rose again, three of those nine were dead and one departed into exile. Yet as she stood in the Bull Court issuing orders to frightened, angry men, her back was straight and her eyes clear, though her face was as white as alabaster.

My father stood next to her, saying nothing. Even though he was Lawagetas, the commander of the military, even though the crew who pursued the Athenians did so in order to avenge the deaths of two of his sons, still he did not offer to command them. He stood there, his eyes empty and dead. No one asked where he was when the alarm was given or how he had come by the angry red scratches that scored his cheek.

Once, I met his gaze. We stared at each other for a long moment and then looked away. I had no desire to betray my father. It would mean his death, or exile at the least. Even though at that moment I did not think he cared much what happened to him, I did not wish to have that on my conscience.

Acalle stood near our parents, looking little altered after her long absence. If she ever learned what part she had played in this drama, would she feel any guilt? I doubted it. She was a practical sort of person.

"Bring me Daedalus the inventor," my mother commanded at last. I closed my eyes and began to pray.

They both came, he and Icarus, though my mother had asked only for the father. I wondered if I might be sick here in front of all these people.

Before my mother could begin to frame a question, Daedalus spoke.

"I gave the key to your daughter Ariadne," he said, "and helped her to arrange their flight. I am sorry for the death of your sons, Queen. That was never my purpose. If I had known that my act would cause you such grief I would never have done it. I submit to anything you think it proper to impose."

"What *was* your pupose, Daedalus?" my mother asked. She didn't sound angry, but only as though it were a question to which she very much wanted to know the answer.

"My mother's sister married the King of Troezen," explained Daedalus. He too gave the impression that he and the queen were having an interesting but not especially momentous discussion. "The boy Theseus is her grandchild. He and I are related by ties of blood."

Something strange seemed to happen to my mother's face then; it sagged on one side. She passed a hand over it and murmured something in an oddly slurred voice that sounded like, "Blood, so much blood . . ."

"It isn't true," someone said loudly. When every eye turned to look at me, I knew that the someone was me.

"I took the key and gave it to Ariadne," I said. "She begged me to. She said she loved him, that she was going to have his baby. So I crept into Daedalus's workshop one day when he was gone and I searched and searched until I found it. It was in a safe hidden in the floor," I added, feeling that this detail might carry conviction. "All that I wanted was that no one should die."

Daedalus shook his head.

"No, child," he said, smiling at me. "You know you're not telling the truth."

I lifted my chin. "You are speaking to the Princess Xenodice, Daedalus," I said coldly. "Do not call me a child."

Icarus laughed. It was a strange laugh, happy and carefree. "But how can we call you anything else, little bird, when you tell such outrageous lies? It was I who carried the key to Princess Ariadne and gave it into her keeping. She thanked me for it very prettily."

"Seize them," came a raven's croak. To my shock, I realized that it was my mother who spoke. "Xenodice —" she faltered, and then continued, "go to your quarters." She staggered, and fell heavily against my father.

He jerked to life. "The queen is ill!" he shouted, and the scene dissolved in confusion.

The dead have been conveyed down into the Underworld with as much ceremony and ritual as we could manage under the circumstances. The potters and stone carvers and goldsmiths and silversmiths worked day and night trying to keep pace with three royal funerals. Normally such a rite would be a major social occasion, with much ostentatious grieving and shows of fine feelings on the part of every ambitious noble family, but no one seemed able to put their heart into it this time. The whole court is distracted, wondering what will happen next.

We have settled into a strange state of suspense. My mother still lives, but she does not speak or move. She cannot last long like this — she can swallow nothing more than a little barley water or wine. Every physician in the land, down to the humblest herbal healer, has offered advice — some maintain that an Athenian enchanter ill-wished her, others that her heart burst from grief. Many sacrifices of rare incense, perfumed oils, cows, sheep, and goats have been offered up to the Goddess, but to no avail. The light in the queen's eye is dimming.

Acalle is beginning to assume the reins of government. She spends much of the day conferring with our mother's counselors. The fool Polyidus is less of a fool than one might think. He sees which way the wind blows and has attached himself to her service with the persistence of a barnacle clinging to a storm-lashed rock. He compliments her beauty and sagacity, runs petty errands for her, pours a steady stream of gossip and malice into her ear, and is clearly planning to carve out an important position as intimate advisor to the next queen. I believe — I hope —

that she sees through him but all the same finds him useful.

She gets no advice or counsel from our father. He has become an old man, shrunken and frail. When she tries to consult with him he waves her away, and she has ceased asking.

Once, only once, did my father speak of what happened the night that Asterius and the others were killed. He was sitting in his chair of state, staring indifferently at the ground, when I came into the room to fetch some embroidery I had left there. I did not trouble myself to offer him obeisance, and he did not comment on my omission. Indeed, I thought that he would let me leave the room without any remark at all, when he spoke.

"I had intended to send Rhesos ahead of Theseus," he began, as though we had been already engaged in conversation on the matter. "He was to remove you from the Bull Pen. That was why I had to have him along to begin with. You would not have been harmed."

"And Catreus and Deucalion? What about Maira and the servant set to watch the door?" I asked, although I knew that those last two deaths weighed lightly on his heart compared to the others. "What plan had you to safeguard them?"

"If only you had not screamed —"

I looked at him with contempt and left the room.

I wondered which of them, Ariadne or my father, had drugged the wine. Perhaps both of them; Rhesos had seemed quite certain that we all should have "slept like the dead." No wonder my glass tasted so foul! Would any of us have ever wakened in the morning had I drunk my share and other events not intervened?

My mother's last words, or very nearly, had been to order Daedalus and Icarus seized. While she hung suspended in this indeterminate state, alive still yet unable to issue further orders, their fate too hung in suspension. No one had the authority to order either their release or their execution, save perhaps my father, and he did not seem to care.

I knew what my sister Acalle would do the moment my mother was cold, because I asked her.

"Execute them, of course," she said. "They have been fed, clothed, and sheltered by our mother's generosity, and now they have betrayed her."

"That was not charity, but payment for services rendered," I reminded her. "You may come to regret the loss of Daedalus's skills. And Icarus too is gifted beyond his years."

Acalle regarded me steadily. "In a land that teems with artists, magicians, and inventors as the sea teems with fish, I do not think we shall even notice the absence of those two traitors. Don't waste my time, Xenodice. They have dug the pit in which they find themselves." And she turned away.

If my mother had not had the fit that now disabled her, the end result might have been different. She had a value and affection for Daedalus that Acalle had not. My mother would have punished him, certainly, after his ready confession. Yet, in the end, I believe she would have set him free. Perhaps he believed it, too, and had relied upon it.

Unlike Theseus, who had been imprisoned in the deepest part of the Labyrinth, Icarus and Daedalus were being held in the highest. Perhaps their jailers reasoned that since being buried deep had not prevented Theseus from escaping, then being raised up to the topmost tower might prove more effective with these prisoners.

There was no particular secret this time; the tower where they were kept was easily seen by all. So I went to visit them, bringing sweetmeats and fruits as in the past I had done for my brother Asterius.

There were guards this time — something had been learned since Theseus's escape. They were polite and deferential to me but would not allow me to enter, permitting me only to call up to the prisoners as they looked out through barred windows above. The little delicacies were examined carefully, as though a key might be baked within a pastry or inserted inside a dried apricot.

A key to the tower existed, but it hung on a ribbon around Acalle's neck, and I knew there was no chance of purloining it. This tower was actually a small edifice perched on top of the seaward walls of the palace; it had been constructed primarily for the purpose of keeping watch over the harbor and the sea. Only occasionally was it put to use as a place of confinement. It consisted of a small room at the top of a winding stair two stories high. The two flights of stairs on top of the five stories of the palace raised the little room up to a commanding height.

I had visited the tower room before — with Daedalus, oddly enough, who had designed and built it. It seemed queer that he should now be imprisoned in his own construction. The place seemed more a part of the sky than of the earth. Standing up there looking out to sea, one had no sense of being in the Labyrinth.

Two shifts of guards sat with their backs to the sole door to the tower every hour of every day. They were not allowed to accept food or drink from anyone, save one servant who had been warned that she would be held accountable if the guards were drugged.

It seemed hopeless.

Icarus was cheerful, waving to me as I parlayed with the guards. Daedalus, on the other hand, was bad tempered and crotchety, though he appeared to hold no rancor against me or mine.

"What news of your mother?" he demanded as soon as I approached.

"She is very ill," I replied. "I do not think that she can get well again."

"I'm sorry for it, Princess," he said gruffly. "She's a good woman, your mother, and a good queen. Besides which, I conclude that our deaths will follow shortly after hers. Ah well, in a way it would almost be a relief, if it weren't for the boy here." Seeing my look of surprise, he grumbled, "Life in this little box is not worth living. I shall go mad if I cannot turn my hand to something. I am not accustomed to idleness."

"It's true," said Icarus. "He complains about his inactivity from morning till night."

"And you, Icarus?" I said shyly. "Are you well?"

"Oh, I am very well. If it were not for my father's distress I would be quite at my ease. I sit and think, you know, and watch the birds."

"Lazy little wretch," Daedalus remarked.

"Yes," Icarus agreed. "I have not your energy. In this situation it is perhaps just as well. I think that the guards grow tired of hearing my father's laments."

I thought hard for a moment, then turned to the guards, who had been quite openly listening to this exchange.

"My mother may die at any moment, or she may yet survive for many days — it is in the lap of the Goddess," I said. "If I were to bring Daedalus one or two things from his workshop so that he would have some occupation, the time might pass more easily for all of you." I added, "You would be very welcome to examine everything I brought, as you have examined the food I brought just now."

The guards looked uneasily at each other.

If there had been a true queen in the palace below us instead of an incapable invalid and an uncrowned girl, I believe that they would not have dared to agree. As things stood, no one seemed to be in charge, and I could see that they, with nothing to do but listen to Daedalus railing against his captivity and lack of employment, would welcome a period of peace and quiet.

"Perhaps — but no knives, my lady," said one of the guards sternly. "I won't be held responsible for allowing prisoners to have weapons."

"No, nor axes, nor scissors, neither," chipped in the other guard. "Nothing with a sharp edge or point, or — or anything that could be *made* to have a sharp edge or point by grinding it against the stones."

"But," I protested, "that would mean that I couldn't bring any tools at all, not a needle for sewing, not even a sharpened stick for drawing on clay tablets —"

"No needles," agreed the guard. "No sharpened sticks."

I turned back to Daedalus, staring at him intently. "Would you like that? If I were to bring you some sort of work from your shop?"

"You would place me, and my son as well, even more deeply in your debt than we already find ourselves, my lady. I would be grateful indeed."

"What would you like? Can you think of anything—?"

"Wait a just a moment, my lady," interrupted one of the guards, looking suddenly suspicious. "Maybe it would be best if the prisoner weren't allowed to specify what, exactly, he's to have. They say he's a clever one." He regarded Daedalus with disapproval.

I bit my lip in disappointment.

"Very well," I said. "Goodbye. I shall return as soon as I can."

I walked slowly and soberly away. Once out of sight of the guards, I began to run.

CHAPTER THIRTEEN

Icarus, Rising

I HAD REMEMBERED SOMETHING ABOUT THAT TOWER ROOM, YOU see, that the guards most likely did not know. Indeed, I thought it unlikely that anyone save we three, Daedalus, Icarus, and me, knew of it, or the tower would never have been thought a suitable prison for the wily inventor.

Daedalus had laid much of the stone of the tower himself, and whatever Daedalus put his hand to always had some distinguishing feature that made it unique. Some rooms he built might have a floor intricately patterned with different-colored blocks of stone, or a window seat, or a built-in stone table with a gaming board inlaid into the top. Quite often he constructed safes like the one in his workshop. I knew he had once or twice built a secret door that could not be detected except by the most determined inspection.

On that day so many years ago, he showed me the secret of the tower room. It was nothing much, only that it was possible, by standing on top of the table that was the sole furnishing of the room, to remove one of the blocks of stone making up the roof. By pushing up on the stone and moving it to the side, a rectangular gap was made in the ceiling, out of which an agile person might crawl onto the very rooftop of the tower.

He had done it in order to extend visibility just a little bit farther; a better vantage point could be achieved by standing on top of the tower rather than inside it. We three had climbed up there that day and sat a little while watching the sun set. Icarus would have liked to stay longer, I know, and I was always happy to be where Icarus was, but after a few moments Daedalus was urging us back inside so that he could busy himself with some new task.

The existence of that loose stone did not compromise the security of the tower as a jail cell for any normal prisoner. A normal prisoner would not know of it, and besides, once on top of the tower there was a drop of three stories to a stone roof or a far greater drop of eight stories to a paved courtyard. No one could survive such a leap uninjured, even if there were no guards below ready to recapture him the moment he landed.

The exit to the roof, therefore, did not solve the problem of how to release Daedalus and Icarus. On the contrary, I could not for the moment imagine how it was to be managed. Still, it offered hope. With a clever mind like

Daedalus's, who knew what might be done? If only he had been allowed to choose what supplies he wanted!

I am no artificer. I could not imagine what sort of equipment would be useful in such a predicament; I could not even guess what most of the things in Daedalus's studio were meant to be used for. The ban on sharp or pointed objects made my choice especially difficult — nearly every tool I could identify as such was either sharp or pointed, or could be made so by grinding it against stone. Once again I searched through Daedalus's belongings, trying desperately to think.

It seemed too great a task. If Icarus and Daedalus could manage to climb down the tower, there were the guards to deal with. And if the guards could be overcome, then I would have to arrange the departure of Icarus and Daedalus from the Isle of Kefti. And if I could do all of this, why then, I had a new cause for sorrow. Because I would lose Icarus as surely as I would if Acalle had him killed. Unless —

Unless I were willing to do as Ariadne had done. Unless I went to Athens with him.

My heart flew up at the thought and then plummeted like a stone. Athens! Exile from Kefti! How could I bear it? Yet how could I bear to part with Icarus?

Sorely troubled, I thrust the subject out of my mind. I

would think on it later. What was required now was a way out of the tower.

I turned my attention back to the contents of the workshop. I wished I was as clever as Daedalus; this conundrum was too hard for my small wits.

At last I thought of the hiding place in the floor. Perhaps there would be something there.

I shifted the sacks of feathers and examined the contents of the safe. Some fine jewelry, cunningly crafted out of gold and silver. A wonderful carving from rock crystal of a griffin. Goblets made from horn. A black steatite vase intricately etched with harvest scenes. Several tools apparently placed here because of their value and rarity, all either sharp or pointed in shape.

I flung myself backward onto the pile of sacks with a groan. There was nothing here that would be of any use in our present dilemma.

As I lay upon the feathers, gazing about me in the languor of despair, my eye fell upon the wooden framework of a wing. Immediately images began forming in my brain.

I saw Icarus and Daedalus standing on the top of the tower, with great white wings strapped to their arms and backs. Daedalus's face was serious and drawn, Icarus's glowed with an internal flame. Daedalus spread wide his feathered arms and launched himself off the tower; Icarus followed. Away they flew, father and son, sailing through the skies like great white eagles, across the sea toward Athens, away from Kefti, away from me.

I sat silent for a long moment. Then I stood up and began to gather together what was needed to build two sets of wings.

The guards eyed my pile of materials. "That Daedalus is a deep one," they murmured to each other. "He's more a magician than anything else, or so they say."

Still, even putting their heads together and thinking hard, they couldn't imagine what mischief Daedalus could devise with several sacks of feathers, a pot of glue, a small quantity of fabric, some leather strips, and a pile of miscellaneous wood pieces — for I had dismantled the frameworks already constructed, in order to disguise their purpose.

"What's this for?" demanded one of the guards.

I had an answer to that question ready.

"I thought that Daedalus, and Icarus too, if he so desires, could make feathered masks for the ceremony of the Blessing of the Boats."

"Hmmm . . ." The Blessing of the Boats was a midsummer ritual marked by much festivity and gaiety — most of the palace-dwellers as well as the residents of Knossos

Town would go masked that night to the celebration after the blessing. The heaps of feathers and wood were far greater than needed for such a task, but I hoped the guards would not realize that.

"Since you are being so kind," I added, "Daedalus might like to give you the results of his labor for the occasion."

"I would indeed," Daedalus called down from the window. I could tell by the emphasis that he had understood the real purpose of my choice of supplies.

"Can't see much harm in that," observed the first guard tentatively.

"Nor can I," said the second, scratching his head.

"Oh, let him have it," said the first. One guard therefore remained at the foot of the tower keeping an eye on me, while the other unlocked the door and toiled up the stairs with the collection.

"I thank you, my lady," Daedalus said, bowing to me through the window. "You are more than kind. This ought to be a sufficiency of materials to complete the task. We are grateful to you."

Icarus poked his head out of another window. "No, father," he said mildly, "You are mistaken. There are feathers enough, but I do not believe that we have an adequate supply of wood. There is a little grove of trees that yields this particular sort of wood — strong, but light and pliable —

just beyond the clearing where we took his Highness, Lord Asterius, to amuse himself not long ago."

He looked at me intently, infusing his next words with meaning.

"I wish to make not two masks, Princess, but three. I would make a mask for you as well, that you might remember my father and me when we are gone. When you wore it, it might seem as though you were still in our company."

I understood him. He was proposing that not two but three sets of wings be crafted, so that I might accompany them in their flight.

"Will you do it, my lady?" he asked.

"I will think on it," I said slowly. "I can promise no more than that."

"And with that I must be satisfied," he replied courteously. "But do not forget that your mother's life hangs by a thread, which may be severed at any moment. If you think too long, the opportunity to give you this material evidence of our love and gratitude may be lost."

I nodded and left them to their labor. I had much to consider.

The most likely outcome of such a mad scheme was destruction. Human beings are not meant to fly through the air. I tried to imagine what such a death would be like. I shuddered to think of the moment of impact. Yet this was a noble doom. I am not beautiful, as I think I have said, but that particular death would make me so — in the tales told afterward, at least.

And if we did not die, if we succeeded? Why, then, I would be a stranger without family or possessions in an alien place where they did not even speak my language, wholly dependent upon Icarus and Daedalus.

Oh, Ariadne! I thought. *What has befallen you, my sister? If I knew your fate I might learn from it to shape my own.*

Yet even as I thought this, I knew that Ariadne's fate, whether good or bad, could be no guide for mine. Icarus and Theseus were two different men, as Ariadne and I were two different women.

Icarus would protect me to the best of his ability in that strange world across the sea. I had no fear of that. But, although he spoke of his love in wishing me to join him, he also spoke of his gratitude.

Ariadne is proud, but in this matter I am prouder still. She did not seem to care why Theseus married her, so long as he did it.

The thought that Icarus might marry me for gratitude alone stuck in my throat like a stone. The suspicion that his every kiss and caress proceeded not from love of me but from a love of his own honor — in time that would kill my happiness. I could be satisfied only by seeing an ardor equal to my own reflected in my husband's eyes.

He loved me, I knew, at least a little. But did he love me enough to quiet my pride?

I would be a burden to him; I could not be otherwise. Life in Athens would be difficult at first; he had never set foot there and knew the language imperfectly. And he was little more than a boy.

If I stayed at home I would be left to face my sister Acalle's anger alone. She would not have me put to death — I was her heir until she married and bore a daughter. But if she learned of my involvement, she would have to take some sort of action against me.

How should I choose? An alien, cold world with Icarus, or a world made alien and cold by his absence?

I did not climb the mountain that day, or the next, or the next. I could allow myself a little time at least, while they completed their own wings. In the torment of my mind I could do nothing but rove the Labyrinth, tracing and retracing its halls.

My mother's condition did not change.

Sometimes I sat in the Bull Pen, looking about and remembering my beloved brother. If I left this place I would be leaving even the memory of him; there would be nothing in Athens to remind me of him. Except Theseus, of course. Theseus, who was to be my powerful brother-in-law in this new life. Could I bear to be a subject in a land whose ruler had killed my poor Asterius?

The wild hatred and despair I had felt on his death had already subsided. Now I sometimes wondered if this were not the best ending for my brother. He had been twelve years old. Soon he would have been a full-grown male, with all the desires and passions of his condition. What would we have done then?

There was little ahead for Asterius but sorrow, I think. So I kissed the ribbons I had been wont to plait into his hair and shed a few brief tears. With all my heart I hoped that he was happy in the Underworld.

On the morning of the third day after I spoke with Icarus and Daedalus, I awoke with a clear mind and a powerful sense of urgency. It was as though a bell had rung in my head. I rose, washed, and dressed. Taking some bread and honey to break my fast, I began to walk toward the mountains as quickly as I could.

I had become possessed of the idea that time had grown dangerously short. Why had I not gone to the mountains yesterday or the day before? Would there be time?

I brought a small saw along with which to cut the saplings. Soon the trail became steeper and the saw banged against the calf of my leg. Sometimes I had to drop to my knees and crawl over steep boulders; I had chosen the shorter but steeper route.

Hurry! Hurry! I knew how foolish I was being. Once I found the grove of trees and cut a sufficiency of branches, those branches would have to be debarked and sawed into appropriate lengths. Then after they were delivered to Daedalus and they were bound into a frame would come the tedious job of attaching the thousands of feathers, one by one. It would take another day, at least.

Yet I knew that I must hurry.

At last, at long last, I reached the clearing on the side of the cliff where we had sat in the sun and laughed at Asterius's antics. How cheerful and content I had been! Now all was in ruins around me.

The trees were those in which the Athenians had waited. I recognized them easily by their slender, whiplike limbs. I began cutting a tree by the very edge of the precipice, dropping branches into a pile by my side.

What made me look over my right shoulder, down into the chasm below?

I don't know. Perhaps it was the memory of the hawk soaring in the updraft on that earlier, happier day.

I saw a man, flying.

He was below me still, but rising rapidly. It was Daedalus, I decided after a little consideration. His body was curled stiffly inward, like a dragonfly in flight. The big white wings did not beat against the air but were held out to the sides, catching the wind like sails.

Once Icarus had pointed out to me how the biggest birds, the eagles and hawks, would use these air currents that rise up the sides of cliffs to elevate their heavy bodies, and that was what Daedalus was doing now. He was close enough that I could just make out the features of his face, though not with any distinctness. I did not think he noticed me. His face was contorted with concentration; he was expending every ounce of energy he possessed to keep himself flying, to keep himself from being dashed onto the rocks below.

I looked down again into the abyss. There was Icarus, flying toward me.

Why did you not wait for me? I longed to berate him for faithlessness, but the blame was mine and I held my tongue. He would not have heard me in any case.

Never had I seen a face so full of joy. *This!* cried his eyes, his limbs, his whole body. *This is what I was born and bred for. This moment and nothing else!*

I knew it was true. His proper fate was not that of an exile, a dutiful husband to a girl without fortune, position, or beauty. No, here was his destiny, this leap into the sky, this gliding through the air.

I rejoiced for him, I swear to you.

He crested the cliff's edge and went on rising. I believe he saw me, for his radiant smile widened.

Dazzled, I dropped my eyes from his glory.

What had happened to Daedalus? A moment later I found him. He had left the rising air currents and was now flying out to sea. He turned and beckoned Icarus to follow him, but Icarus was not attending.

Icarus went on and on, up and up.

At last he was nothing but a speck of darkness in a brilliant blue sky, headed straight into the sun.

I could look no longer; tears blinded my eyes. I nearly missed seeing the last of him. As he rose higher and higher, I suppose that the heat of the sun began to melt the waxen glue that bound the feathers to the frame. The frame itself disintegrated.

He spun around in a wide spiral and fell — not back to earth but into the sea. I was glad of that at least; it seemed a cleaner death.

Daedalus came back and flew laboriously in a circle, once, twice over the sea where Icarus fell, looking for signs of life. Then he flew away.

Sometime later a messenger arrived, out of breath from the climb.

"My lady! I am sorry, my lady," he panted, "but the queen orders your attendance upon her immediately."

"The queen?" I asked. I looked up at the man, startled out of my lethargy.

"Queen Acalle," he explained, embarrassed. "Your lady mother is dead and your sister Acalle is now queen."

"I see," I said. "I will come."

Ariadne, Descending

LAST NIGHT I SAW MY SISTER, WHO IS DEAD. SHE STOOD AT THE end of a long corridor, weeping.

I did not know her until I drew near. There are some here in the Labyrinth who are strangers to me. I thought her a new servant beaten for disobedience, and I looked at her closely only when she did not move as I approached.

Her body was just beginning to be big with child, a child who never saw the light of day. Her neck was encircled by the rope with which she had hanged herself, yet her face was not distorted and discolored, as the faces of the hanged are, and I could see her features clearly.

"Can it really be you, Ariadne, come back after all this time?" I whispered.

She did not answer, but began slowly to sink through the floor.

I am a dignified and important person now, but I ran like the girl I once was to the nearest stairway. I wished to see if my sister's feet would appear on the ceiling of the story below. I descended a few steps and looked to see.

They did. My sister was drifting downward through solid stone.

I glanced around to see if anyone else saw what I saw. But no, I was alone. At this hour few walked these hallways in the nether regions of the queen's quarters. I ran down the rest of the stairs.

"Tell me, sister," I adjured her, after waiting until her head had fully emerged from the ceiling. "What is your will?" She did not speak but wept silently.

As I watched, fascinated, she revolved twice in the air, as a leaf will when it falls. Still she sank, until she began to descend through the next floor.

"Ariadne," I protested, "I —" Her head slipped beneath the stone. I hurried down the next flight of stairs. There were two more floors below us. When she dropped through the last floor it would be into the earth and I would see her no more.

"It is I, Xenodice," I called out. "You fall faster than I run. Stop!"

Her face changed a little then. She made a slight gesture, as of one who says, "I cannot."

"Well, then, fall more slowly," I panted, rounding the turn of the stairs.

It appeared that Ariadne was able to stay her downward movement a little. She flowed through the next floor like honey through a sieve.

I pattered down the last staircase. As I arrived, gasping, before my sister, I saw her beginning to sink through the floor and into the ground beneath. She had disappeared almost up to the knees.

Seeing that I had no time to waste, I at once asked, "Why do you come to me, Ariadne? If you wish to atone for your crimes, you perhaps should plead your cause before Acalle, who is now queen." Thinking that she might not know, I added, "Our mother is dead, and our father also. Three of our brothers —" I broke off and then continued awkwardly, "But of course you knew about those deaths. Do you . . . do you ever see them there, where you are?"

Her head drooped so that her chin touched her chest. The floor had reached her waist now.

They tell us that the Underworld is a place of joy and harmony. My sister did not appear to have found it so. But then, mine was a tactless question; none of my family would be likely to greet Ariadne in the afterlife with great enthusiasm. I should not have mentioned them.

Her breast was now at the level of the floor.

"Our brother Glaucus is to marry Semele of Phaistos in

the springtime," I said quickly, hoping to cheer her. "You remember Semele. You never liked her, I know, but I believe that they will be happy together. They both like to eat so much. Oh, and little Phaedra is to marry —" I broke off with a blush. Of course she did not want to hear about our little sister Phaedra's wedding plans.

Her face and what remained visible of her body convulsed with emotion and she shook her head "no," her movements as slow as those of a swimmer suspended in deep waters. I cursed myself for my stupidity.

"Do not go, Ariadne," I said. I spoke with urgency now, for only her head remained above the floor. "You have not told me what you require of me." I remembered that she had been buried in foreign soil, without a tomb or the tribute of grave goods.

"Is — is there anything that you need in the afterlife, Ariadne? Tell me and I will make certain that you get it. Only — only Acalle must not know." Her mouth and nose had vanished; her eyes alone beseeched me, for what I did not know.

"Come back!" I cried. "Come back! I —"

My voice trailed off into silence. She was no more.

I whispered, "I — I miss you, Ariadne," but no one heard, and no one answered.

* * *

It was not until nearly a year after Ariadne fled with Theseus that we learned what had happened to her. Receiving official notice that Theseus was to be married, we were merely surprised they had delayed so long — until we heard the name of the bride: Hippolyta, Queen of the Amazons. Only then did we discover that he had deserted Ariadne on the Isle of Naxos many months before.

Some said that it was an accident. Because of her condition (she was right about bearing his child), she had felt the movement of the ship more grievously than most. She begged, they said, to tarry at Naxos for a time, waiting for the seas to subside. Theseus was willing, all the more so as it meant that the pursuing Keftiu sailed right past them, unseeing. Ariadne slept ashore, while Theseus and his Athenians remained on board the ship in a small harbor on the lee side of the island.

A dreadful storm blew up one night and carried Theseus and his compatriots out to sea. It was fifteen days and fifteen nights before he regained the shore again. By that time Ariadne had abandoned herself to despair, believing him to have sailed off to Athens without her, and had laid violent hands upon herself.

Or so they said.

It is also recounted how Theseus, when he had sailed from Athens to our shores, made a promise to his father,

Aegeus, that if he were able to return he would raise aloft a white sail. In this manner Aegeus would know, while Theseus was still at sea, that his son lived.

Theseus broke his promise. He sailed into Athens harbor in a ship with black sails, forgetting in the excitement of homecoming to exchange them for the white symbols of hope. Aegeus saw the ship from the Isle of Kefti fully rigged in black, and in his grief he flung himself over the cliffs into the sea.

So Theseus became king of Athens.

It is a matter of some amazement to me how that man strides unscathed through life, leaving a trail of the maimed and the dead.

It is many years now since that time. Much has changed. My father, King Minos, is gone into the Underworld. My mother's death seemed to stir him from his long torpor and, upon learning that Daedalus had fled across the sea, he sailed in pursuit. He traced Daedalus finally, not to Athens as I had expected but to Kamikos in the western sea — the winds, I suppose, blew him there. My father was greeted with honor by the king of that land, who promised to surrender Daedalus to him. My father slipped in his bath and fell while preparing to appear at a banquet in his honor, breaking his neck.

Or so they said.

I am glad, at any rate, that Daedalus lives still.

Acalle is married and has five children, three girls. Polyidus died, apparently in a fit of mortification at being denied the position of High Priest for which he had schemed so long. Many others, more greatly mourned than he, have followed him into the Underworld: my beloved old Graia, for one.

Athens has grown prosperous under Theseus's rule. No longer just a pirate state, Athens is beginning to exert power among the nations of the world.

Acalle wishes to marry Phaedra, now grown to womanhood, to Theseus, since his first wife, the Amazon queen, is lately dead. This marriage, which would have been unthinkable only a few years ago, is beginning to seem a likely event. Acalle is a businesslike and efficient queen; she wants favorable trade relations and cares not a fig for revenge.

Theseus is no longer a young man but an experienced ruler of full years. I hope it will be for Phaedra's happiness — those who love Theseus seem to come to untimely ends. I despair of ever making Acalle listen to my fears about the marriage. I have done what I can to sway her, but she is a stubborn woman, and she is the queen.

And I, Xenodice. Do you wonder what has become of me down the long years?

I lead a quiet life today, respected and, I believe, loved. The love I enjoy is not the love of a man for a woman; I have never had that love and have vowed that I never shall.

I have become Mistress of the Animals, a priestess of influence and power, thereby escaping my elder sister's marriage schemes. The Mistress of the Animals may not marry, nor may she invite any man to share her bed. She is chaste and pure, and much beloved of the Goddess.

I spend my life now in the mountains among the wild beasts, or in the Queen's Menagerie, which I have expanded greatly. Little Queta the monkey has become the matriarch of a vast tribe of tricksy, troublesome descendants, and we now possess animals unknown to us only a few years ago. My sister presently owns (though the knowledge does not seem to give her much joy) a hippogriff and a mighty elephant from the wild places far to the south of Libya and Egypt. The hippogriff is sickly and has developed a hollow cough in the night, but the elephant does well. I would like to obtain a mate for him and see what result we have. A baby elephant would please me very much.

My health is excellent, though my wrist never fully healed; it aches sometimes, and I favor that hand. It may seem strange, but when the rainy season comes and I feel the familiar pain in my left arm, I am glad. It is one of the few mementos I have of my brother Asterius.

I think of Icarus often. In my mind he remains young and beautiful, while I grow old and fat. Never mind — I am happy, even though he took my heart with him into the sea that day.

It took Acalle very little time to determine my part in the escape of Daedalus and Icarus. When questioned, the guards told her how I had come to visit the prisoners, bearing feathers, wood, and wax. I confessed as quickly as possible in order to save the lives of the guards. They were beaten nearly to the point of death, but they survived. One lived for a year, dying from a bee sting; the other still lives.

Daedalus and Icarus kept their word. They left three exquisite feather masks there in the tower room; I use mine for the ceremony of the Blessing of the Boats every summer, as does the remaining guard.

As punishment, Acalle locked me up in that same tower for a year and a day. It was just; I have no complaint.

I learned to live alone during that year; I learned to be self-sufficient. Now when I come down from the mountains I seem to live in a positive hive of activity among my animals and my nieces and nephews — so much so that I sometimes yearn for the peace and quiet of those lonely days.

I regret nothing, though I grieve for much.

I only wish I knew what my sister wanted to tell me.

Author's Note

In the year 1900, the ruins of an enormous, labyrinthine palace of immense antiquity were uncovered on the island of Crete in the Mediterranean Sea. The Palace of Knossos (or Cnossos) and the civilization that created it quickly became associated with the Greek legend of the maze and the Minotaur. These fabulously wealthy and sophisticated people are known today as the Minoans, after King Minos of myth.

This book is an attempt to reconcile the archeological findings with that myth.

The story we know was first written down by an Athenian, Apollodorus, who lived sometime between 100 and 200 A.D. The civilization on Crete reached its peak of power and influence around 1700 B.C.E. (before the Christian, or Common, Era). The events in this tale therefore occurred nearly 2,000 years before Apollodorus was born. It is almost certain that the narrative altered somewhat during that time, over the course of countless retellings.

My version of this story differs in several ways from those told by Apollodorus, Ovid, and other writers. In most cases, the differences stem from the difficulty of making the myth fit some of the facts we now know about ancient Crete. Because so little of the written language of ancient Crete survived, there is much about this society that we do not know and that I have therefore invented.

For instance, it is possible but by no means certain that these people were ruled by a queen rather than by a king. The archeological record does seem to suggest that women had a great deal of power, and the myth itself implies that Queen Pasiphae was well able to protect herself and her strange offspring the Minotaur from a husband who could not have been pleased by the birth.

No one today knows exactly what the inhabitants of ancient Crete called themselves. We do know that their contemporaries, the Egyptians, referred to them as the "Keftiu," and their land "Kefti," or the "Island of Kefti," so that is what I have called them here.

Some archeologists believe that ancient Crete was actually the lost island of Atlantis, which Plato tells us sank under the sea after a terrible cataclysm. In 1450 B.C.E. the island Thera, a close neighbor and a colony of Crete, was blown to bits by a violent volcanic eruption. The clouds of ash, tidal waves, and earth tremors resulting from this explosion apparently toppled palaces on Crete, sank her ships, and blighted her agriculture. Within fifty years, mainland Greeks had seized control of Crete and one of the world's most remarkable civilizations was no more.

Legend tells us that Xenodice's little sister Phaedra married Theseus in his old age. She then fell in love with his son by an earlier marriage. When her stepson refused to return her love, Phaedra killed herself, leaving a letter accusing him of assault. Theseus sent his son into exile with a curse on his head, and the young man died soon afterward.

Reason enough for Ariadne's warning from beyond the grave, even though it proved to be as ineffectual as warnings from beyond the grave usually are.

Genealogy

Royal Family of the Palace of Knossos (NAH-sus or k'no-SOS)

Minos (MEE-nos or MY-nuhs) — Pasiphae (pa-sif-AY-ee) — The Bull in the Earth

Minos and Pasiphae: Androgeus (an-dro-JEE-oos)

Pasiphae and The Bull in the Earth: Asterius (as-TER-ee-us)

Androgeus (an-dro-JEE-oos)
|
Acalle (ah-ka-LEE)
|
Catreus (KAT-ree-oos)
|
Deucalion (doo-KAY-lee-on)
|
Ariadne (ah-ree-AD-nee)
|
Xenodice (zen-OH-dih-see)
|
Glaucus (GLAW-kuhs)
|
Phaedra (FAY-drah or FEE-drah)
|
Molus (MOLE-us or MAH-lus)

Royal Family of Athens

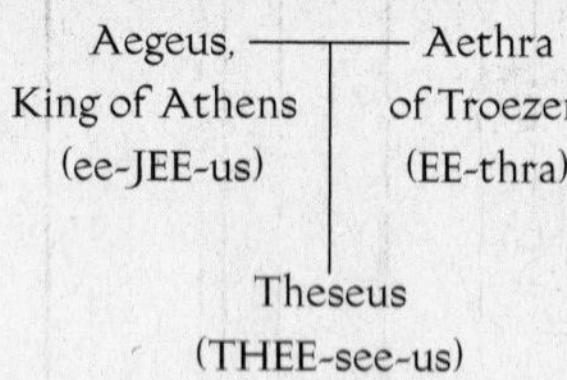

House of Daedalus

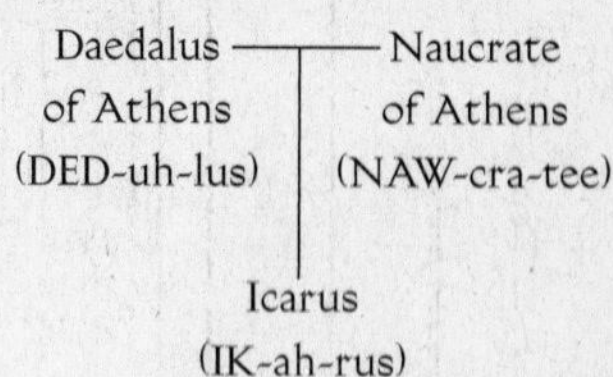

Further Reading

On the subject of Greek mythology, two adult books are Edith Hamilton's *Mythology* (Boston: Little, Brown, 1942) and Mary Renault's *The King Must Die* (New York: Pantheon, 1958). For children's books on this subject, see *A Gift from Zeus: Sixteen Favorite Myths* (New York: HarperCollins, 2001),written by Jeanne Steig and illustrated by William Steig, and *Greek Myths* (Boston: Houghton Mifflin, 1949), written by Olivia Coolidge.

Unfortunately, many of the books available on ancient Crete have lots of footnotes and few illustrations. However, I do recommend *The Knossos Labyrinth* (London: Routledge, 1989) and *Minoans: Life in Bronze Age Crete* (London: Routledge, 1990), both by Rodney Castleden.

Two good web sites are www.historywiz.com, a handsome site with basics of Minoan civilization and illustrated with Minoan art, and www.wsu.edu:8080/~dee/MINOA/MINOANS.HTM, a site created by Washington State University, with more text and fewer illustrations. These can also be found by searching using the keyword "Minoans."